The Short Stories
of
Sean O'Faolain

The Short Stories
of
Sean O'Faolain

A Study in Descriptive Techniques

Joseph Storey Rippier

COLIN SMYTHE
GERRARDS CROSS 1976

D.30

First published in 1976 by Colin Smythe Ltd.
Gerrards Cross, Bucks.

ISBN 0 901072 30 3

All quotations are included by kind permission of Sean O'Faolain

342256

Produced in Great Britain.

for
Professor Willi Erzgräber
In Gratitude

Introduction

Much good work has already been done both on the short story and on Sean O'Faolain's short stories.

Maurice Harmon's book on Sean O'Faolain[1] is, and will no doubt remain for some time, the standard work. Harmon has sensitively and penetratingly written about O'Faolain's achievements, interpreting these in terms of O'Faolain's beliefs, technique, and his attitude to Ireland past and present. He includes an excellent bibliography, as does Paul A. Doyle[2] in his book.

There have been several recent dissertations. Susanne Dockrell-Grünberg[3] has selected eight Irish writers (George Moore, James Joyce, Mary Lavin, Michael McLaverty, Liam O'Flaherty, Frank O'Connor, Bryan MacMahon, Sean O'Faolain) and has taken one story from each as a basis for an explanation of the development of the modern Irish short story. Although she says at the beginning that her main aim is merely to establish general and common features, her analyses of the stories bring out a number of individual characteristics as well. She has also assembled a very extensive bibliography on the short story.

Catherine Murphy's[4] long section on Sean O'Faolain is divided into three chapters in which she looks at the way politics, religion, and Irish life and character are reflected in his stories. Miss Murphy sees the stories consistently and "dominantly concerned with the imperative within the individual, of self-realization and fulfilment in the face both of natural limitations and man-made social forces which act to oppose this imperative" (p. 5). By working with examples from the stories Miss Murphy is able to provide convincing evidence to support her arguments.

Two other studies have dealt with the Irish background of O'Faolain stories[5] while Pauline Dalton[6] has examined O'Faolain's narrative skills.

In the course of reading into the subject I noticed that although most critics refer to O'Faolain's narrative techniques, often interpreting these at length, there appears to be no study in which O'Faolain's use of language, particularly of descriptive language, is analysed, except in terms of specific stories. For that reason I felt it might be helpful if a discussion of O'Faolain's descriptive techniques was linked with examination of diction.

By working closely with the text I have tried to understand and explain why O'Faolain employs language in a particular way. I have constantly borne in mind the dictum that there must be harmony between the language of a short story and what that story is to portray. I have looked carefully at the presentation of character, nature, emotion, perspective, attempting to appreciate what effect the writer wishes to achieve through the words he chooses.

I have generally taken words at their face value, interpreting them from the context. At the same time, where it has been possible to refer to other stories, in which certain patterns or similarities might be noted (for example, in the presentation of nature), I have not hesitated to do this, in the hope that comparison should lead to greater clarity.

The selection of stories is arbitrary but not random, and was made from work published over a long period. Most of the stories, on closer examination, reveal common features (for example, of plot, character, narrator, or setting) so that continued examination of these features in consecutive chapters may again serve to show more clearly developments in O'Faolain's technique. Only a few stories were chosen, so that in some cases an almost word-for-word analysis has been possible. I quote extensively from the stories, and also from other short-story writers. I try to employ the quotations as part of a general argument. As the study proceeds, I sometimes place the same quotations from early stories beside similar passages from later ones, attempting to understand O'Faolain's diction in something other than the isolation of individual stories.

I have tried to see the stories through the eyes of "the common reader". For that reason, while attempting to go deeper, I have first looked for the reasons and need for descriptive words at the surface level. In cases of metaphor, I have striven to understand it in terms of the objects to which it refers.

There has been no attempt to set up, or rely on, a specific stylistic theory. It has been my constant endeavour to read the descriptive words within their context and to evaluate their effect from this. Where terminology adopted might have been confusing I offer explanations. While I realise that terms such as "cliché" or "metaphor" have been the subject (rightly) of controversy, for the purpose of this study I have been content to accept definitions, for example of these two expressions, provided by Alex Preminger[7] :

Metaphor : A condensed verbal relation in which an idea, image, or symbol may, by the presence of one or more other ideas, images, or symbols, be enhanced in vividness, complexity, or breadth of implication.

Cliché : A phrase or figure which from over-use, like a dulled knife, has lost its cutting-edge; a trite expression.

In these introductory remarks I wish to stress once again that descriptive words cannot be considered by themselves, as standing outside the text in which they appear. As I hope to show, in the short story above all, descriptive language is a major, though often cleverly disguised, part of the whole.

NOTES

[1] Maurice Harmon, *Sean O'Faolain, A Critical Introduction*, London : University of Notre Dame Press, 1966.

[2] Paul A. Doyle, *Sean O'Faolain*, New York : Twayne Publishers, 1968.

[3] Susanne Dockrell-Grünberg, *Studien zur Struktur Moderner Anglo-Irischer Short Stories*, Diss. Tübingen, 1967.

[4] Catherine A. Murphy, *Imaginative Vision and Story Art in Three Irish Writers: Sean O'Faolain, Mary Lavin, Frank O'Connor*, Diss. Dublin, 1967/68.

[5] Annie Pianezza, *The World of Sean O'Faolain's Stories*, Diss. Lille, 1969.

[6] Joanne Trautmann, *Counterparts: The stories and Traditions of Frank O'Connor and Sean O'Faolain*, Diss. Indiana, 1967.

[6] Pauline Dalton, *The Narrative Art of Sean O'Faolain*, Diss. Leeds, 1972.

[7] Alex Preminger, ed., *Encyclopedia of Poetry and Poetics*, New Jersey : Princeton University Press, 1965.

Contents

Editions of O'Faolain's Works Used and Abbreviations Adopted

                Abb

Midsummer Night Madness and Other Stories, MNM
London : Jonathan Cape, 1932

A Nest of Simple Folk, London : Jonathan Cape, 1933

Bird Alone, New York : Phaedra, 1969

A Purse of Coppers, New York : The Viking Press, 1933

Come Back to Erin, London : Jonathan Cape, 1940

The Man Who Invented Sin, New York : Devin-Adair, 1949

The Short Story, New York : Devin-Adair, 1964

The Finest Stories of Sean O'Faolain, New York : FS
Bantam, 1965

Short Stories, A Study in Pleasure, ed. Sean O'Faolain,
Boston : Little, Brown and Co., 1961

I Remember! I Remember, London : Hart-Davis, 1962

The Heat of the Sun, Stories and Tales, London :
Pan, 1966

The Talking Trees and Other Stories, London :
Jonathan Cape, 1971

Abbreviations of Stories

"Midsummer Night Madness"	MNM
"Admiring the Scenery"	ATS
"Lady Lucifer"	LL
"Up the Bare Stairs"	UTBS
"The Silence of the Valley"	SOV
"The Trout"	TT
"Lovers of the Lake"	LOL

Early Stories I

THE INTEGRATION OF DESCRIPTIVE TECHNIQUES

Many of the great writers of short stories have stressed the care which must be exercised in the choice, placing and harmony of words in an art form which might, for intensity of effect, be compared with chamber music. The essential limitations on length mean that every word must justify its presence or be ruthlessly excised. It would be foolish to maintain that such extreme standards are achieved often, but, as the following quotations show, they are standards towards which all the recognised masters of the modern short story have striven.

> The writer's problem of language is the need for a speech which combines suggestion with compression. (Sean O'Faolain, *The Short Story*, New York : Devin-Adair, 1964, p. 217).

> No matter what we want to say, there is only one noun to denote it, one verb to animate it, and one adjective to qualify it. We must therefore seek until we have discovered that noun, that verb and that adjective, and never content ourselves with an approximation, or resort to fraud, however clever, or clownish tricks of language to avoid the difficulty. (Guy de Maupassant, Int. *Pierre et Jean, and Selected Short Stories*, New York : Bantam, 1969, pp. 13–14).

> In your search for the best way to express your ideas, always be guided by Pushkin's golden words : "Precision and brevity are the prime qualities of prose." Babel paused and suddenly, with a smile . . . added : "Only don't think it's all that easy, precision and brevity. That's the most difficult thing, much more difficult than writing beautifully." (Isaac Babel, *You Must Know Everything*, London : Joanthan Cape, 1970, pp. 272–273).

In the Foreword to the *Finest Stories*, O'Faolain again refers to the difficulty of simplicity :

> I must, if only in self-defence, tell the reader of this volume that it opens with three stories from my first book of stories, *Midsummer*

13

Night Madness, and that although I have chosen them because I
like them very much they contain things that make me smile today
– and, yet, I have been unwilling to re-write them. I should like
to explain why. They belong to a period, my twenties. They are
very romantic, as their weighted style shows. I should have to
change my nature if I were to change the style, which is full of
romantic words, such as "dawn", "onwards", "youth", "world",
"adamant" or "dusk"; of metaphors and abstractions; or personalizations and sensations which belong to the author rather
than to the characters. They also contain many of those most
romantic of all words, "and" and "but", which are words that are
part of the attempt to carry on and expand the effect after the
sense has been given. Writers who put down the essential thing
without any cocoon about it, do not need these "ands" and "buts".
The thing is given and there it lies; whereas the writer who luxuriates goes on with the echoes of his first image or idea. His
emotions and his thoughts dilate, the style dilates with them, and
in the end he is trying to write a kind of verbal music to convey
feelings that the mere sense of the words cannot give. He is chasing
the inexpressible. He is interested mainly in his own devouring
daemon. He is, as I was when I was in my romantic twenties,
drowned in himself. (p. vii).

O'Faolain, however, finds himself in an uncomfortable situation.
While he admires the French for their unflinching honesty and
clarity of expression, and while he praises Hemingway for his "genius
for seizing the essential", he is still unable to accede to the austerity
of these models.

I cannot help thinking that the factually meticulous realistic
style is a step backwards technically ... though, in my taste, it is a
brutal and spiritless and sluggish weapon at all times. Wherever
there is wit, or an imaginative stir of humour or passion, or concentration of feeling or observation, we will find the more suggestive language leaping across deserts of literalness, and we chase
after it to its glittering oasis ... For, it does not matter in what
school a writer establishes himself, his language must, under challenge, expand its normal voltage by becoming, in the literal sense,
more radiant, throwing off new extensions of meaning like an
exploding star, if he will but let it – if he has the passion to make
it do so. The besotted realists, like Zola, never could do this. (*The
Short Story,* p. 233).

.Throughout his book on the short story O'Faolain uses words like
"dilation", "suggestion" and "implication", to put his finger on the
point at which the magic must begin to work.

There never will be one ultimate prescribed manner in which a short story – or for that matter, any form of literature – is to be written. But whatever technical, stylistic or aesthetic approach a writer adopts, his aim is to offer his vision of truth and that can only be attained by a single-minded pursuit of the one and only way to express what he wishes to say. In an interview, Faulkner emphasizes this point :

> The aim of every artist is to arrest motion, which is life, by artificial means, and hold it fixed so that a hundred years later when a stranger looks at it, it moves again, since it is life. (*Writers at Work: The Paris Review Interviews*, New York : The Viking Press, 1958, p. 139).

Since a writer works with words, the language he uses must carry the truth – or at the very least, some of the truth. Words can of course be bent and twisted to mean many things. There may also be hidden meanings which the words will not openly convey, as often happens in allegory, for example. Other meanings may also emerge if a story can be read at more than one level, as in "The Silence of the Valley", in which O'Faolain is not really writing about the characters who appear in the story, but of the dead tradition of Irish story-tellers. In such an instance, examination of the language will be seen to have its limitations. But even a story with that under-swell of meaning will not stand the test of time if the words the writer uses do not tell the surface story appropriately. There must be harmony of language and content, a drawing together of all that is essential.

Such considerations are not necessarily confined solely to the short story. They can have equal relevance in other art forms. For example, in talking about Constable, Kenneth Clarke says :

> It is this sense of dramatic unity, as much as his feeling for the freshness of nature, which distinguishes Constable from his contemporaries. He recognized the fundamental truth that art must be based on a single dominating idea and that the test of an artist is his ability to carry this idea through, to enrich it, to expand it, but never to lose sight of it, and never to include any incidents, however seductive in themselves, which are not ultimately subordinate to the first main conception. (*Landscape into Art*, Boston: Beacon Press, 1963, p. 76).

Similarly in poetry, Ezra Pound draws up the following "rules" for Imagists :

Use no superfluous word, no adjective which does not reveal something. Don't use such an expression as "dim lands *of peace*." It dulls the image. It mixes an abstraction with the concrete. It comes from the writer's not realizing that the natural object is always the *adequate* symbol.

Go in fear of abstractions. Do not retell in mediocre verse what has already been done in good verse. Don't think any intelligent person is going to be deceived when you try to shirk all the difficulties of the unspeakably difficult art of good prose by chopping your composition into line lengths...

Use either no ornament or good ornament. (*Modern Poets on Modern Poetry*, ed. James Scully, London : Fontana, 1966, p. 32).

One way of discovering what a writer is attempting to do with language is to compare the original manuscript with the finished work. It was not possible to do this for the purpose of the present study. However, careful study of the first edition of "Midsummer Night Madness" and the version which appeared much later in *The Finest Stories of Sean O'Faolain*, shows that alterations have been made. In a letter on these alterations, O'Faolain said that, " . . . any changes in the text were made by me" (letter dated 12 October 1973). It will be obvious that examination of these changes, made so many years after the story was written, will provide a helpful basis from which to work towards an understanding of how O'Faolain uses language. In the Foreword to *The Finest Stories* he himself refers to the excessive number of "ands" and "buts" in the original version. Many of these are removed from the later edition. Some slight changes have also been made to "Fugue". The other stories are reprinted as they were in the original. The changes consist largely in excisions, re-arranging of paragraphs, replacement of certain words, different spellings, altered punctuation, some few additions, and the removal of the original section-markings (I, II, III).

Only in the presentation of the narrator is it possible to see that slight modifications in character have been attempted. In the original version, the narrator is more hesitant, shy, even prudish. O'Faolain must have later felt that this was not really in keeping with the man who had been sent out from headquarters to discipline Stevey Long.

A certain moralising tone is softened in the revised version : (words bracketed have been removed in *The Finest Stories*.)

FS

(pp. 2–3)   (Clearly, a) A man who lived by the things of the body.. (*MNM*, p. 5).

He was one of the class that had battened for too long

on our (poor) people. I was (quite) pleased to think that if he lived (only in name) he lived only in name; that if he had any (charm at all'left) physique left now he would need it all (now) to attract even the coarsest women. (For no) No London light-o'-love would be attracted to his ruin of a house now for other reasons(.); (Perhaps he was beyond all that, and if he was not, he would be like Juan in old age, for) the farmers' daughters for miles around would shun him (as they would) like the plague(,); and (for such a man as Henn to descend to the women of the passing tinkers for whom alone his house would appear even yet a big house was out of the question. And yet not) even (his) maids who came from a distance would not be in the (house) place a day without hearing all about him from the neighbours. Perhaps(, after all, the tinkers) the travelling tinker-women would have to suffice? (*MNM,* p. 9).

(p. 5)

(p. 9) I wished Stevey would turn to see me (sneering) looking at him. (p. 16).

(p. 9) "Was, eh, was Henn down tonight, Gyp?" (I could see her turn towards me as she answered with a brazen "No". Then she said under her breath to him.) "He knows what he'd get if he came." (p. 16).

(p. 12) I returned, (no doubt a little flattered, but) largely because I did not know what else to do . . . (p. 21).

(p. 13) "Why are you in this business, tell me?" he asked of a sudden. (I . . .) I believe in it," I said (awkwardly). (p. 22).

(p. 14) "Your people were merchants," I said (rather timidly) coldly. (p. 23).

(p. 14) I saw for the first time how deep the hate on his side could be, as deep as the hate on ours, as deep and terrible (, and although he angered me there was so much contempt in his face and voice that I could scarcely muster up the courage to meet his eyes. His whisky was rising in my head.). (p. 24).

(p. 19) . . . I thought he might not have quarrelled with old Henn if he (knew) had known I was there. (So) I stood . . . My hopes of a quiet, serene night were (already) vanished (, and I felt to Stevey as one feels towards some hooligan who breaks in on lovely music with his loud shouting and laughter.). (p. 31).

(p. 20) . . . calling him . . . a lunatic(;) and (he would not deny he was) a libertine (as well). p. 33).

B

(p. 21)	(But) I did not tell her that the name was well-known in North Cork for a tinker tribe . . . (a name few decent men or women ever bore). (p. 34).
(p. 24)	(I was, I admit, a fool that night.) (p. 38).
(p. 24)	Then, (But) slowly, I understood . . . (How stupid I had been – but) Such reprisals were as yet rare in the country . . . (p. 39).

Two further purposes are served by the removal of words and phrases in the later version. The narrator takes several steps backwards, is thus de-personalised to a greater extent. He still tells the story, but the author lets the facts speak for themselves much more. The second advantage is that a certain knowledgeability exuded by the narrator is eliminated.

FS

(p. 3)	It was only one of many such escapades that (my mother knew, all) spread(ing) the name . . . (*MNM*, p. 6).
(p. 3)	. . . and went in mortal terror of him and his salting for years. (No wonder we . . .) We used to say . . . (p. 6).
(p. 3)	It was a wonderful old house to look at, (and often we looked at it from far off), sitting . . . (p. 7).
(p. 6)	"Henn was down again tonight. Stevey, I . . .' (Astonished, I made no sound) The rain beat down . . . (p. 10).
(p. 6)	"What a rough (passionate) creature!" I was saying to myself (only by degrees recovering from my surprise) as I began to wheel my bicycle up the avenue when I heard her steps behind me (and felt her grip on my arm once more). (p. 11).
(p. 7)	. . . I looked into her face by the light of the little window, (as one always looks into the face of a person one doubts) . . . (p. 12).
(p. 9)	I had something to go on already, (I thought,) and I was . . . (p. 16).
(p. 11)	(And as I said nothing the) The shuffling came nearer . . . (p. 19).
(p. 11)	"I don't quite understand," I said, and mentally cursed Stevey for not having arranged things better (than this for me). (p. 19).
(p. 18)	But his voice trembled as if he were half afraid of his own daring. (Well he might.) (p. 29).
	(Only a)A shaft of wavering light lay thrown across

(p. 22)   the tiny hallway from another room. (Moving cautiously to the other window I peered in again.) There they were, Gypsy and Henn . . . (p. 36).

(p. 23)   . . . he caressed and caressed and looked and looked dog-like into her face (Alas! each exhausted sigh was but the prelude to a new shuddering burst of tears like waves that are silent for a while and then burst suddenly and inevitably on the shore). (p. 37).

(p. 25)   (But I was concealing something from her and she would not believe me) There was no sound from the house. (p. 40).

(p. 25)   . . . Gypsy shook him madly into a gasping wakefulness, (and seeing me, in the faint glow that filled the room, smile at his comically stupid look she) straightened his cap . . . (p. 41).

(p. 26)   (But when I tried to lead him back to the bed he) He flung my arm aside, peevishly. (p. 42).

There are occasions in the first version when the narrator appears to have more knowledge than could logically be expected. At his first meeting with the gypsy girl he says :

(p. 6)   She beckoned and drew me back into the shadow of one of the sheltering trees beside the little house, (and with the only grace she was capable of leant) leaned insinuatingly close to me, fingering my lapel, and said in (her) a hollow mannish voice: (p. 11).

(p. 6)   Her voice was strained against the leash (, become passionately intent in spite of her). (p. 12).

In one or two other passages, there are personifications which have later been eliminated :

(p. 7)   The wind shook the heavy leaves . . . the light from the little Gothic window shone on (their) these wet leaves . . . (p. 12).

Occasional Irishisms are also removed :

(p. 15)   It was a long-drawn-out "Ah!" of (the) sweet memories. (p. 26).

One or two mistakes in logic have also been corrected in the later version :

(p. 6)

. . . I began to wheel my bicycle up the avenue (,) when I heard her steps behind me. (*and felt her grip on my arm* once more.) She *beckoned* and drew me back . . . (p. 11).

(p. 13)

. . . and his rug trailing after him on the *uncarpeted* floor. I sat by the table and looked about me again : at the table-cloth like a gypsy's shawl, (at the *thread-bare carpet on the floor*,) . . . (p. 21).

In a further instance O'Faolain shifts a phrase from the end of a paragraph to the beginning. This occurs on the first page of the story, and again, the passage becomes much more logical. Originally the passage read :

> *Then I turned to the open fields* and drew in a long draught of their sweetness, their May-month sweetness, as only a man who had been cooped up for months past under one of those tiny roofs, seeing the life of men and women only through a peephole in a window-blind, seeing those green fields only in the far distance from an attic skylight. *Mounting my bicycle* I left the last gas-lamp behind, and the pavement end, and rode on happily in the open country. (*MNM*, p. 3).

Later this becomes :

> Then, mounting my bicycle, I turned to the open fields . . . (*FS*, p. 1).

which makes much more sense, since otherwise the text would suggest that he walked to the outskirts of town before getting on to his bicycle.

On the next page there is one more alteration in the arrangement of sentences. This time it can only have been done for effect, since there is no change in meaning. In the original the passage reads :

> *And all about me the dead silence of the coming night*, unless a little stream trickled over the road and my wheels made a great double splash as they crossed it; then once again *the heavy silence, drowsy with the odours of the night flowers and cut meadows.* (*MNM*, p. 4).

Later this is changed to :

> *And all about me the dead silence of the coming night, the heavy*

silence, drowsy with the odours of the night flowers and the cut meadows, unless a little stream trickled over the road and my wheels made a great double splash as they crossed it. (*FS*, p. 2).

In the rearranged passage one is immediately struck by the rhythmical effect of placing the word "silence" twice in a repetitive sequence, coupled with words which are powerful in their emotive impact.

A number of single words have been altered, generally for reasons of greater clarity and accuracy :

FS

(p. 3)	The (place) facade was a pale rain-faded pink (*MNM*, p. 7).
(p. 5)	. . . that if he had any (charm) physique left now . . . (p. 9).
(p. 23)	(For somehow) Suddenly country and freedom seemed . . . (p. 37).
(p. 33)	We drove the rest of the (herd) chaps before us into the darkness (so) now rain-arrowy . . . (p. 53).

Occasionally a repetition, or romantic expression, is changed :

(p. 11)	. . . and only the old tireless (croaker) corncrake . . . (p. 18).
(p. 17)	. . . (the swan's neck) his lean neck curved . . . (p. 28).

Sometimes, as has already been seen, the change transfers attention away from the narrator's point of view :

(p. 19)	She was (strangely) entirely cool . . . (p. 31).

or results in the reader gaining a different impression of the narrator :

(p. 14)	I said (rather timidly) coldly. (p. 23).

In one instance a phrase, "a tinted London beauty" (*MNM*, p. 5), is later changed to "a tinted London trollop" (*FS*, p. 2). "trollop" has possibly been inserted here because of what immediately precedes : "But, judging by his later life, he cannot have been overparticular at any time in his choice of women." The author must have felt that "beauty" was too neutral a word.

The sentences in the first edition of "Midsummer Night Madness" are often very long. Within the sentences, phrases and clauses tend to be linked by series of "ands". Many sentences and paragraphs begin with "and" or "but". In the later edition such linking words are often removed. The sentences become shorter :

FS

(pp. 1–2)

Yet though the countryside was very sweet to me after all those months among the backyards, I was worried and watchful lest I should run into a chance patrol or raiding-party (,). I kept listening, not to the chorus of the birds, not to the little wind in the bushes by the way, but nervously to every distant, tiny sound – the chuckle of a wakeful goose or hen in a near-by farm-yard, or the fall of water coming suddenly within ear-shot, or some animal starting away from the hedge where I surprised its drowsing heavy head (, and once). I halted dead, my grip tight on the brakes when a donkey brayed suddenly and loudly as if he were laughing at the intense quietness of the night. Fallen hawthorn blossoms splashed with their lime the dust of the road, and so narrow were the boreens in places that the lilac and the dog-rose, hung with wisps of hay, reached down as if to be plucked (, and under). Under the over-hanging trees I could smell the pungent smell of the laurel sweating in the damp night (–) air. (*MNM*, pp. 3–4).

The effect of the full-stops is to make a natural break, so that the reader's attention is drawn to something new.

It will later be necessary to look again at the first version, to decide whether the long, rambling sentences were, as O'Faolain suggests, just the result of "trying to write a kind of verbal music", or whether there may not be some model on which such stylistic devices are based. It is certainly true that at times when there is more action, the shortening of sentences seems more appropriate.

FS

(p. 11)

A door opened again (and steps). Steps shuffled along the passage and halted; . . . (*MNM*, p. 18).

(p. 17)

He did not see me (at first, and he approached). He gave the old man (with) a low "Good night" (and I thought the long neck drew into itself again.) p. 28).

(p. 17)

Her sullen eyes (were) went soft (and in). In this light she looked almost beautiful. (p. 29).

(p. 20)

Gypsy returned (, and). I told her I was staying . . .
(p. 33).

(p. 21)

The pair and their song died slowly (, and when).
Then silence (fell Henn). Henn kicked his enamel
chamber-pot until it rang. (p. 35).

(p. 23)

I could not bear those dog-like eyes of the old libertine,
nor those sighs and sobs of the young girl (; and
stumbling). Stumbling away from the light of the little
window . . . (p. 37).

(For somehow) Suddenly country and freedom seemed
a small thing under this austere darkness with that
pair, heavy with one another's sorrow, down in the
weather-streaked decaying cottage (; and with).

*With the memory of those drooping mother's
breasts and that large mother's belly on the young
girl, and the look of pity on the old libertine's face, I
find myself walking aimlessly on and on† (.) ; until
(But suddenly) across the black valley there rises a
leaping yellow flame, and through the night air on the
night wind comes the crackle of (the) burning timber
(, joists moist with the damp of years, burning the
vermin in their cracks and the resinous veins.).

The flames through the trees (flickered) were now
flickering like a huge bonfire (and running). Running
down the lanes toward Henn Hall I could see from
time to time as I ran the outline of windows (of) a
gable-end, (of) a chimney silhouetted against the glowing air (about it). At the lodge the little light was still
shining in the window (but without). Without looking
through I knocked and knocked until bare padding
feet came along the floor and the girl's voice said . . .
(p. 23)   (MNM, pp. 37–38).

In both versions there are three paragraphs. Originally the reflec-
tions on the sight of the incongruous pair were contained in the first
paragraph, leaving the other two to the description of the fire. The
reason for the change may be found in the changes of tense. In the
later version there is a switch from the past tense in the first, to the
historic present in the second, back again to the past in the third
paragraph. The effect of these paragraphs is much improved as a
result of the re-structuring. Through the elimination of some words
and phrases, the passage – particularly the part describing the fire
– becomes much clearer, and has no need of additional detail. This

*New paragraph in later version.
†New paragraph in first version.

becomes particularly clear when one looks at the removal of the last part of the sentence in the second paragraph ("joists moist with . . .").

In the last paragraph O'Faolain has changed the tense to the past continuous, presumably to keep the sense of immediacy; possibly also because he continues with a further -ing form.

Other changes in tense are to be found in the course of the story :

(p. 8)   . . . the great dark cypresses (might) in the wet failing light (have been) were plumes . . . (p. 13).

The change here makes the description much more direct, turns a comparison into a metaphor.

On two occasions present tenses are changed to past ones :

(p. 13)   . . . and I (remember) remembered the look of the yards . . . (p. 21).

(p. 34)   But I (find) found it too painful to think of him . . . (p. 55).

The present tense in both cases comes after descriptive passages in the past, and draws unnecessary attention to the narrator. It is not essential that the reader should give any thought to what the narrator now thinks about the sight of the strange pair wandering through the streets of Paris. That is something which the reader can be left to do for himself. These changes of tense may once again be seen as deliberate attempts to ease the narrator towards the back of the stage.

In the case of the second sentence it is necessary to quote the passage in full, because there are further changes at the end – not only of tense, but also in the words used.

(p. 34)   But I (find) found it too painful to think of him (, there in Paris,) with his scraps of governess-French, guiding his tinker wife through the boulevards, the cafés, the theaters (–), seeing once more the lovely women (and the men) gay in their hour. (Life is too pitiful in these recapturings of the *temps perdu*, these brief intervals of reality.). Anyway, we had more important things to think of then. (p. 55).

The use of a past tense here minimises the narrator's presence, a process which is continued by the substitution of an almost cheeky throw-away final statement for the original, which is literary, and trite. The first ending unnecessarily comments on Mad Henn and his relevance in the story. The second, by refusing to do more than just describe Henn's appearance in Paris, leaves it to the reader to draw his own conclusions.

Examination of additions, alterations and excisions so far has shown that these are aimed at simplifying and intensifying what O'Faolain wishes to say. Passages which "carry on and expand the effect after the sense has been given" are removed.

Certain changes in descriptive passages bear this out:

(p. 4)	. . . and the flooded river ran frothing and brown (and storm-blown) . . . (p. 8).
(p. 4)	At the same time the cold, yellow sky behind it was turning to a most marvellous red as of blood, and the scarlet light blackened every leafless twig and (already rain-black and rain-green) tree-trunk that stood against it . . . (p. 8).
(p. 5)	. . . the tenting chestnuts filled the lanes with darkness (as of pitchy night), and under my feet . . . (pp. 9–10).
(p. 10)	. . . listening to the corncrake at his last dim rattle in the meadows, and the doves fluting long and slow in the deep woods (through the fallen dark). (p. 17).
	. . . the dark figures gathered about us again (, like wolves, or tormenting flies that had been driven aside for the moment). (p. 49).

Elsewhere, allusions to music, literature and classical figures are removed or modified:

(p. 5)	(Perhaps he was beyond all that, and if he was not, he would be like Don Juan in old age) (p. 9).
(p. 9)	Stevey burst suddenly into a wild roar of song, his old favourite ("Night of Stars and Night of Love"), the barcarol(l)e from Hoffmann . . . (p. 16).
(p. 21)	"Questo é il fin di chi fa mal . . ." (E de' perfidi la morte, alla vita è sempre ugual!") (p. 35).

The deleted sentence at the end of the story with the Proustian reference has already been mentioned.

Other deletions indicate a desire to avoid unnecessary repetitions or additions:

| (p. 2) | . . . my mother always spoke of him as "that old divil" (or "that old cripple") of a Henn. (p. 5). |

(p. 17)   . . . (and I thought the long neck drew into itself again) . . . (p. 28).

(p. 17)   As their eyes met (the swan's) his lean neck . . . (p. 28).

sometimes, an obvious dissatisfaction with the expression :

(p. 22)   . . . her fallen lashes on her cheeks, (her parted lips that never moved) . . . (p. 36).

(p. 22)   . . . her breasts like tulips fully blown, if anything too magnificently full, (too Jewess soft,) . . . (p. 36).

(p. 28)   . . . and all about him shouted with him out of the dark (in their rough country accents) . . . (p. 45).

(p. 28)   . . . the big houses looked on in portly indifference. (Again and again they echoed it back to him.) (p. 46).

(p. 29)   . . . You (blasted father of thousands) . . . (p. 47).

(p. 31)   . . . he had leant across the shining walnut to his (perfumed) lights-o'-love . . . (p. 49).

(p. 31)   . . . he offered his smoke-tainted tea (, with the airs of fifty years ago, though they creaked and stuttered a little from lack of use) to the two . . . (p. 50).

(p. 32)   (As the) The girl wept with renewed shame that no man would own (now that he ever loved) her (,). (p. 52).

(p. 33)   . . . trying once more to play the host (after his fifty years' interval), . . . (p. 53).

One piece of information is withheld in the later version :

(p. 27)   Gypsy is going to be a mother (next month or after). (p. 44).

O'Faolain must have decided that it was better to leave out such precise information. It is not important to know when the girl will have her baby, but merely that she is going to have one. Up to this point O'Faolain just hints at the girl's condition. Not until near the end does Henn actually say that the girl is pregnant. It is only later that the reader appreciates the irony of the way O'Faolain describes the girl when she meets the narrator at the begininng of the story :

(p. 7)   For a second I thought her blue apron drooped over her too rich, too wide hips . . . (p. 12).

These are the major changes to "Midsummer Night Madness".

Similar, though fewer, alterations can be discovered in the two editions of "Fugue".

"ROMANTIC" INFLUENCES

In the Foreword to the *Finest Stories*, O'Faolain says his first stories :

> . . . are very romantic, as their weighted style shows. I should have to change my nature if I were to change the style, which is full of romantic words, such as "dawn", "dew", "onwards", "youth", "world", "adamant" or "dusk"; of metaphors and abstractions; of personalizations and sensations which belong to the author rather than to the characters. They also contain many of those most romantic of all words, *and* and *but*, which are words which are part of the attempt to carry on and expand the effect after the sense has been given.   (p. vii).

Comparison of the two editions has already shown that by removing many of the "ands" and "buts", O'Faolain has also eliminated passages which add nothing to the sense, or passages in which the reader is expected to share too much in the narrator's attitude towards the other characters and in what is happening, or sections in which the author feels the narrator obtrudes.

O'Faolain uses the words "personalizations, sensations, metaphors and abstractions", to describe the Romantic style in which he wrote these first stories. Perhaps one could amplify this definition, to try to establish what the word "Romantic" may be taken to mean when applied here. The definition offered by Wellek and Warren in *Theory of Literature* will be adopted :

> Romantic description aims at establishing and maintaining a mood : plot and characterization are to be dominated by tone, effect . . . (René Wellek and Austin Warren, London : Peregrine, 1966, p. 221).

In "Midsummer Night Madness" there is the strong suggestion of the cleansing, purifying quality of the countryside; in "Fugue", constant reference to the eternal rhythm of the seasons, the harmony of traditional life in the country. These are ideas which found favour with writers of the Romantic period and with the writers who gathered around Yeats. A number of Romantic themes can be noted : the seasons, nature, love, death, youth, revolution, nostalgia for past civilizations, idealism.

Ireland, at the period in which this story is placed, is struggling for independence. The young revolutionaries and artists of the time wished to re-create a culture which had been stamped out centuries before. There is the strong suggestion in much writing of the period that in the countryside, where life had gone on relatively undisturbed down the centuries, elements of that ancient culture still existed. The narrator in "Midsummer Night Madness" was brought up in the country, and so might be said to be returning to his real home when he leaves the town.

These points may not seem to have a direct relevance to the present discussion. However, before going on to look more carefully at the language used in this story, it is necessary to try to appreciate why a certain kind of language should be adopted. The French Revolution was anticipated by some of the Romantic writers. Ireland's revolution came over a century later. It roused native writers in a similar way. That their writing should contain rather more than just echoes of the language used by Romantic poets is only natural.

Just how strong these associations are, may be seen by placing a passage from the beginning of "Midsummer Night Madness" beside lines from "Ode to a Nightingale" by Keats.

Yet, though the countryside was very *sweet* to me after all those months among the backyards, worried and watchful lest I should run into a chance patrol or raiding-party, I kept listening, not to the *chorus* of the birds, not to the little wind in the bushes by the way, but nervously to every distant, tiny sound – the *chuckle* of a wakeful goose or hen in a near-by farm-yard, or the *fall of water* coming suddenly within ear-shot, or some animal starting away from the hedge where I surprised its *drowsing heavy* head, and once I halted *dead*, my grip tight on the brakes when a donkey brayed suddenly and loudly as if he were *laughing* at the *intense quietness of the night. Fallen hawthorn blossoms splashed* with their *lime* the dust of the road, and so narrow were the *boreens* in places that the *lilac* and the *dog-rose*, hung with wisps of hay, reached down as if to be *plucked*, and under the over-hanging trees I could *smell the pungent smell* of the laurel *sweating in the damp night-air. And all about me the dead silence of the coming night,* unless a little stream trickled over the road and my wheels made a great double splash as they crossed it; then once again the *heavy silence, drowsy with the odours of the night-flowers and cut meadows.* (*MNM*, pp. 3–4).

But here there is no light,
Save what from heaven is with the breezes blown
Through *verdurous glooms* and *winding mossy ways.*

I cannot see what flowers are at my feet,
Nor what *soft incense* hangs upon the *boughs,*
But in *embalmed darkness,* guess each *sweet*
Wherewith the *seasonable month endows*
The grass, the thicket, and the fruit-tree wild;
White hawthorn, and the *pastoral eglantine;*
Fast fading violets cover'd up in leaves;
And *mid-May's eldest child,*
The coming m*usk-rose,* full of *dewy wine,*
The *murmurous haunt* of flies on summer eves

Darkling I listen; and for many a time
I have been half in love with *easeful Death,*
Call'd him soft names in many a *mused rhyme,*
To take into the air my quiet breath;

("Ode to a Nightingale", 38–54)

Certain parallels may be noted even in the subject-matter of both
works. In his interpretation of "Ode to a Nightingale", Richard
Fogle says that it is :

. . . a Romantic poem of the family of "Kubla Khan" and "The
Eve of St Agnes" in that it describes a choice and rare experience,
intentionally remote from the commonplace. (*Englische Lyrik von
Shakespeare bis Dylan Thomas,* ed. Willi Erzgräber, Darmstadt :
Wissenschaftliche Buchgesellschaft, 1969, p. 280).

"Midsummer Night Madness" could also be described in such
terms. The narrator's experiences at Henn's house are extraordinary.
The house and all that surrounds it seem to be outside the rest of the
world. Fogle continues :

Nowadays we sometimes underrate the skill required for this
sort of thing. The masters of Romantic magic were aware that
ecstasy, for example, is not adequately projected by crying, "I am
ecstatic !" Keats gets his effects in the "Nightingale" by framing
the consummate moment in oppositions, by consciously emphasizing its brevity; he sets off the ideal by the contrast of the actual.
The principal stress of the poem is a struggle between ideal and
actual : inclusive terms which, however, contain more particular
antithesis of pleasure and pain, of imagination and commonsense
reason, of fullness and privation, of permanence and change, of
nature and the human, of art and life, freedom and bondage,
waking and dream. (Ibid, p. 280).

All these oppositions may also be found in the story, the only difference being that they are shown in more concrete terms through characters who are identified, whereas Keats is concerned almost exclusively with ideas and emotions. This can be seen even more clearly when such concepts as age, youth, beauty and love are taken. Keats presents these by means of personifications. O'Faolain, in the characters of Henn, the narrator, Stevey, Gypsy, and in the relationship between Stevey – Gypsy, Henn – Gypsy, uses the same material, although he works it very differently. There is nothing idealistic about the affair between Stevey and Gypsy, or even, in the beginning, between Henn and the girl. It is a grotesque reversal of the ideal concept of love. Even when the old man decides to marry the girl, this will be felt to be nothing more than a maudlin act, the result of senility.

Both the passages quoted contain words which describe states rather than precise objects. Keats transports the reader into a mood of dreamy wakefulness, the mind intoxicated by verse which seems inexhaustible in its sensual variety. O'Faolain uses the section quoted – and others in the story – to take the reader into the mind of the narrator. One is made aware of the refreshing effect of coming out into the country from the stifling confinement of a room in the city. At the same time, O'Faolain does not go as far as Keats in "crushing the grapes of language on his palate and luxuriating in a magic world of dream and sorrow and sensation!" (David Daiches, *A Critical History of English Literature*, London : Secker & Warburg, 1963, Vol. 2, p. 921). Where Keats can say :

> I cannot see what flowers are at my feet...
> ... but in embalmed darkness guess such sweet,

O'Faolain leaves one in no doubt as to what he sees, hears, smells and feels around him in nature. There is a skilful combination of vague Romantic vocabulary with clearly defined objects.

As Fogle points out :

> The "Nightingale" does not seem a notably pictorial poem; in it the associations of objects are much more important than their outlines...
> The forest scene is Romantically picturesque without being really pictorial : one does not visualize it, but its composition is describable in visual metaphor...
> The imagery is particular and sensuous, but not highly visual.
> (*Englische Lyrik von Shakespeare bis Dylan Thomas*, pp. 284–5)

Keats talks of "verdurous glooms", "soft incense", "embalmed darkness", "pastoral eglantine", "mid-May's eldest child", "the coming musk-rose". Most of these expressions do not describe so much as imply, inspire emotional response. O'Faolain also uses vague adjectives like "sweet"; "intense" (darkness), "dead" (silence), "heavy" (silence), "drowsy with the odours of the night flowers and cut meadows". However, O'Faolain demonstrates that he is not thinking of some undefined "mossy way", but of a particular road leading out of Cork. The details of objects seen along the road are stated: the goose, the donkey, the smell of leaves. Implicit in this passage and in later ones is the presentation of the fecundity of nature, of all things bursting with life – as a contrast to the sterility of the city. This is what O'Faolain means when he talks about language dilating, going beyond the surface meaning of the words. Even so, most of the descriptive words and images conjure up things which one can see in the mind; they do not just provoke a desired emotional response. It is "fallen" hawthorn blossoms; the dog-rose is not qualified at all. The narrator refers to the wisps of hay which hang from it. He observes, records. O'Faolain might be seen as following the Chekhov dictum that

> . . . a true description of nature should be very brief and have a character of relevance . . . (p. 70).
> Descriptions of Nature must above all be pictorial, so that the reader, reading and closing his eyes, can at once imagine the landscape depicted; but the aggregation of such images as the twilight, the sombre light, the pool, the dampness, the silver poplars, the clouded horizon, the sparrows, the distant meadow, – that is not a picture, for however much I try, I can in no way imagine all this as a harmonious whole. (*Checkhov Letters on the Short Story, The Drama, and Other Literary Topics*, ed. Louis S. Friedland, London : Vision Press, 1965, p. 74).

The descriptions of nature in this story are not particularly short, but there can be no doubt of their relevance. O'Faolain selects the small details which make the scene live. Furthermore, where he uses more ambitious expressions like the blossoms "splashed" in the dust, or the laurel leaves "sweating" in the night air, he intensifies the effect by using tangible metaphor. The passage as a whole leads up to the final onomatopœic, alliterative ending:

> . . . heavy silence, drowsy with the odours of the night-flowers and cut meadows.

Throughout this story and others in the first collection many

Romantic expressions will be found. Reference to the Concordance for example, reveals a whole battery of Keatsian expressions employed by O'Faolain in "Midsummer Night Madness" :

> starry, sweet, drowsy, soft, pale, rough, passionate, darkling, full, rich, billowy, wild, deep, lovely, graceful, serene, white, warm, dark, black.

It cannot be pretended that these words are the exclusive property of Keats, since many other Romantic and later poets (for example Yeats) also used them. Nevertheless there are some phrases in "Midsummer Night Madness" which may well have their origin in Keatsian idiom :

> the tenting chestnuts filled the lanes with darkness . . .
> into the darkness now rain-arrowy and cold . . .
> From my bed I heard the summer downpour drip . . .

Keats :

> Underneath large blue-bells tented . . .
> Fan-shap'd burst of blood-red arrowy fire . . .
> Like rose-leaves with the drip of summer rains . . .

So far, certain terms have been used in an attempt to define the kind of language used by Keats and O'Faolain. But these words themselves : "vague", "Romantic", "pictorial", "visual", must be adopted with care. All of them are frequently found in the most disparate of contexts, and even in applying them to Keats and O'Faolain, it may still not be clear what is meant by Romantic allusive (Keats) as opposed to Romantic visual (O'Faolain). It has to be admitted that there are problems in attempting to establish parallels between "Romantic" writing in poetry and "Romantic" elements in prose, since the Romantic poets do not appear as a united, uniform group. Perhaps it will be helpful to refer to Ruskin's remarks on "The Pathetic Fallacy". In discussing good and bad poets, Ruskin says that :

> The greatness of a poet depends upon the two faculties, acuteness of feeling, and command of it. (John Ruskin, *Modern Painters*, Vol. III, London : George Allen, 1904, p. 173).

Ruskin continues :

> So, then, we have the three ranks : the man who perceives

rightly, because he does not feel, and to whom the primrose is very accurately the primrose, because he does not love it. Then, secondly, the man who perceives wrongly, because he feels, and to whom the primrose is anything else than a primrose : a star, or a sun, or a fairy's shield, or a forsaken maiden. And then, lastly, there is the man who perceives rightly in spite of his feelings, and to whom the primrose is for ever nothing else than itself – a little flower apprehended in the very plain and leafy fact of it, whatever and how many soever the associations and passions may be that crowd around it. (Ibid, p. 168).

Kenneth Clarke takes up the yardstick offered by Ruskin, and, employing the third approach, applies it to the Italian painter, Bellini :

He chooses, to symbolise his subject, the moment when the plain is still in shadow, but the rising sun has touched the hill-tops. Deeply imaginative as it is, this effect is also perfectly true, as anyone who has visited the walled towns of the Veneto will remember, and it is clearly the result of impassioned observation. Bellini's landscapes are the supreme instance of facts transfigured through love. Few artists have been capable of such universal love, which embraces every twig, every stone, the humblest detail as well as the most grandiose perspective, and can only be attained by a profound humility. (*Landscape into Art*, p. 24).

Even if O'Faolain says in the Foreword to the *Finest Stories* that he now "smiles" at the Romantic language he finds in the early stories, it is possible to justify this language, to see why it does what is asked of it, and also how, as a result of being combined with more precise diction, a successful fusion is achieved of the language the writer employs with what he wishes to portray.

OTHER POSSIBLE INFLUENCES

Comparison of the early and later editions of "Midsummer Night Madness" showed that changes had been made. To consider how O'Faolain constructed his sentences, it will be necessary to return to first edition :

Yet, though the countryside was very sweet to me after all those months among the backyards, worried and watchful lest I should run into a chance patrol or raiding-party, I kept listening, *not* to the chorus of the birds, *not* to the little wind in the bushes by the way, *but* nervously to every distant, tiny sound – the chuckle of a wakeful goose or hen in a near-by farm-yard, or the fall of water coming suddenly within ear-shot, or some animal starting away from the hedge *where* I surprised its drowsing heavy head, *and* once I halted dead, my grip tight on the brakes *when* a donkey brayed suddenly and loudly *as* if he were laughing at the intense quietness of the night. Fallen hawthorn blossoms splashed with their lime the dust of the road, *and* so narrow were the boreens in places *that* the lilac and the dog-rose, hung with wisps of hay, reached down as if to be plucked, *and* under the over-hanging trees I could smell the pungent smell of the laurel sweating in the damp night-air. *And* all about me the dead silence of the coming night, *unless* a little stream trickled over the road and my wheels made a great double splash as they crossed it; *then* once again the heavy silence, drowsy with the odours of the night-flowers and the cut meadows. (*MNM*, p. 3–4).

Now a similar passage from "Fugue" :

We had tramped up and down *and* up and down until I felt my eyes closing as I stumbled along, *and* scarcely had the energy to push back my bandolier *when* it came sliding around my elbows. Rory, a country fellow, seemed tireless, *but* my shirt clung to my back with cold sweat. The fog lay like a white quilt under the moon, covering the countryside, *and* black shadows miles long and miles wide stretched across the land. Up and down we went, the fog growing thicker as we stumbled into boggy valleys, our feet squelching in the sodden turf, and fear hovering round our hearts. Earlier in the evening, before the night fell, I had heard a noise before us in the lag, *and* had clicked a bullet in my rifle-breech *and* fallen flat, *but* Rory swore at me *and* asked me in amazement *if* I meant to fight them? After that I had no guts for anything *but* to get away from the danger of an encounter, to get across the river and the main road *before* the dawn, *and* up to the higher mountain on Ballyvourney beyond. *So* we trudged on *and* every natural night sound terrified us, a bird's cry, a barking dog with his double note, bark-bark, *and then* silence, bark-bark, *and* like that now and again the whole night long from one mountainside or another. People say the most lonely thing of all is the bark of a dog at night, but to us the most lonely sight was the odd twinkle of a light, miles away, one dot of light *and* all the rest of the land in darkness, *except* for the moon in the sky. The little light meant friends, a fireside, words of advice *and* comfort – *but* for us only the squelching and the trudging *that* never seemed to end, *and* maybe a bullet in the head before the dawn. (*MNM*, pp. 66–67).

It is possible of course that the preponderance of "ands" and "buts" and other linking words in these passages is purely fortuitous, or that O'Faolain did not realise he was writing in this particular fashion. However there is also the possibility that he was, consciously or unconsciously, imitating a device affected by two other Irish writers – Yeats and Moore. In Moore's story, "Home Sickness", such passages occur frequently. For example :

He was sorry he did not feel strong enough for the walk, the evening was fine, *and* he would meet many people coming home from the fair, some of whom he had known in his youth, *and* they would tell him *where* he could get a clean lodging. *But* the carman would be able to tell him that; he called the car *that* was waiting at the station, *and* soon he was answering questions about America. *But* he wanted to hear of those *who* were still living in the old country, *and* after hearing the stories of many people he had forgotten, he heard *that* Mike Scully, *who* had been away in a situation for many years as a coachman in the King's County, had come back *and* built a fine house with a concrete floor. Now there was a good loft in Mike Scully's house, *and* Mike would be pleased to take in a lodger. (*Modern Irish Short Stories*, ed. Frank O'Connor, London : Oxford Univ. Press, 1957, p. 2).

In *Autobiographies* Yeats points out that :

Style was his (Moore's) growing obsession, he would point out all the errors of some silly experiment of mine, then copy it. It was from some such experiment of mine that he learnt those long, flaccid, structureless sentences, 'and, and and, and and'; there is one of twenty-eight lines in *Muslin*. (*Autobiographies*, London : Macmillan, 1956, p. 438).

In the same book, however, Yeats too indulges in the same kind of "structureless" sentence :

Some of my misery was loneliness *and* some of it fear of old William Pollexfen, my grandfather. He was never unkind, *and* I cannot remember that he ever spoke harshly to me, *but* it was the custom to fear *and* admire him. He had won the freedom of some Spanish city, for saving life perhaps, *but* was so silent *that* his wife never knew it till he was near eighty, *and then* from the chance visit to an old sailor. She asked him if it was true *and* he said it was true, *but* she knew him too well to question *and* his old ship-mate had left the town. (Ibid, p. 6).

It is doubtful whether Yeats or Moore gains anything by adopting this rather monotonous device. In the Moore passage, the removal of most of the "ands" and "buts" would be no loss. There is no particular advantage gained by stringing the clauses together in what, on closer examination, appears to be a merely haphazard pattern. It is not as if just one person is talking all the way through. Moore begins by describing the thoughts of Bryden, using the third person. One hears what others tell him in the course of his first evening in Ireland, and that he is offered accommodation in a loft. There is no feeling that the unusual frequency of "ands" and "buts" is anything but artificial. Susanne Dockrell-Grünberg offers an explanation :

> Durch diese im regelmäßigen Wechsel erscheinende Aufteilung ergibt sich ein ruhig fortschreitender Rhythmus. (*Studien zur Struktur Moderner Anglo-Irischer Short Stories*, Diss. Tübingen, 1967, p. 18).

This is true. It is nevertheless a mannered rhythm which seems to have no particular connection with the story as such – unless as a useful contrast to more active passages, as Mrs Dockrell-Grünberg suggests :

> Nur die beiden vorletzten Abschnitte weisen kurze Sätze auf und entsprechen der beschriebenen Hast und Raffung der Ereignisse. (Ibid, p. 18).

However this would merely appear to confirm the artificiality of the method. There is no evidence that it is essential to the story.

In the passages by O'Faolain it is possible to find an explanation for the long sentences, and for linking these with conjunctions. In the first, the writer is describing the thoughts of somebody who is riding slowly out into the country. It is action of a sort, but it is not action which needs demonstrating through a series of short sentences. There is tension, but no real danger. Therefore the passage proceeds in lengthy sentences. A sense of motion is maintained at a steady pace through to the end. The "ands" and "buts" have the effect of creating the impression that one is accompanying the narrator. Each little incident is related briefly, with a smooth transition to the next. At the beginning, where there is an occasional moment of nervousness for the narrator, the text is stopped short within the sentence by "or", repeated three times, before it moves on again.

The second O'Faolain passage is also interesting in this respect, because here one might have expected shorter sentences. There is action. The two men are on the run; they are fired on. However, it is not action which O'Faolain is trying to present, but the mental state of two very tired fugitives. The constant repetition of "and" helps to bring this home. Of course the details of what lies around the two men are also important in this passage, but nevertheless, the lengthy sentences linked by "ands" and "buts" set up a rhythm which fits in with what is happening in the story, particularly since the action is now over.

A different kind of effect, using the same device, can be seen by looking at a paragraph from a novel by Hemingway :

It was a warm spring night *and* I sat at a table on the terrace of the Napolitain after Robert had gone, watching it get dark and the electric signs come on, and the red and green stop-and-go traffic-signal, *and* the crowd going by, *and* the horse-cabs clippety-clopping along at the edge of the solid taxi traffic, *and* the poules going by singly and in pairs, looking for the evening meal. I watched a good-looking girl walk past the table *and* watched her go up the street *and* lost sight of her, *and* watched another, *and* *then* saw the first one coming back again. She went by once more *and* I caught her eye, *and* she came over *and* sat down at the table. The waiter came up. (Ernest Hemingway, *Fiesta*, London : Jonathan Cape, 1964, p. 20).

The narrator is sitting outside a cafe, recording what he sees. Harry Levin, in discussing passages which are written in this way, says : "If beauty lies in the eye of the beholder, Hemingway's purpose is to make his readers beholders." ("Observations on the Style of Ernest Hemingway", in *Hemingway and His Critics*, ed. Carlos Baker, New York : Hill & Wang, 1961, p. 108). Levin also talks about Hemingway's "sequence of motion and fact". The motion in the present paragraph is merely that of the series of small happenings which are connected by the regular, insistent use of "and", sometimes "and then". "Hemingway holds the purity of his line by moving in one direction, ignoring sidetracks and structural complications." (p. 109). The text does not read naturally. It is not meant to. The presentation is deliberate; it nevertheless has purpose. Levin quotes Robert Jordan : "You feel . . . that all that happened to you." (p. 108). Nothing must come in the way of the direct contact between the text and the reader. For this reason Hemingway is sparing in the use of adjectives. Where he does insert qualifiers, they tend to be of a kind which do not describe. The reader has to imagine what is intended. For example in the passage quoted, there are expressions like : "warm", "spring", "solid", "good-looking". Levin mentions other adjectives : "fine", "nice", "good", "lovely", which he says do not describe, but evaluate.

Unlike Moore, Hemingway often uses the repeated "and", "and then" device in passages which describe action, in order to achieve immediacy. It happened in this way, and in this sequence. Flash, flash, flash.

It is only in the early stories that O'Faolain introduces long, apparently structureless sentences. As has already been seen, he later removed many of the conjunctions to shorten his sentences.

There is a further point of view from which the deliberate and regular use of the same conjunctions must be considered : repetition. Starting with George Moore, many Irish writers (and later, writers like Hemingway and Faulkner) frequently constructed passages in which certain key words would be found repeated, not always in the same way. A word might appear as adjective, later as noun, verb or adverb. Joyce took this device as far as – perhaps further than – was possible. In *A Portrait of the Artist as a Young Man*, there is the following extraordinary paragraph :

A *girl* stood before him in midstream, alone and still, *gazing* out to *sea.* She seemed like one whom magic had changed into the likeness of a strange and beautiful *seabird.* Her *long* slender *bare* legs were delicate as a *crane's* and pure save where an emerald trail of *sea*-weed had fashioned itself as a sign upon the flesh. Her thighs, fuller and *softhued* as ivory, were *bared* almost to the hips where the *white* fringes of her drawers were like featherings of *soft white* down. Her slateblue skirts were kilted boldly about her waist and *dovetailed* behind her. Her bosom was as a *bird's soft* and *slight, slight* and *soft* as the breast of some darkplumaged *dove.* But her *long* fair hair was *girlish* : and *girlish*, and touched with the wonder of mortal beauty, her face. (*Portrait*, London: Jonathan Cape, 1968, p. 175.

Frank O'Connor, in commenting on such passages, talks in terms of "mechanical writing", explaining that :

. . . deliberate repetition of certain key words, sometimes with a slight alteration of form . . . produces a peculiar effect that is not the result of precise observation, but of a deliberately produced hypnosis. (*The Mirror in the Roadway*, London : Hamish Hamilton, 1957, p. 296).

In connection with the Joyce passage quoted, O'Connor continues :

I find it difficult to transcribe, let alone analyze, the passage because it seems to me insufferably self-conscious . . . I suspect there are at least two movements in a passage of this sort, one a local movement that seems to rise and fall within the framework of the paragraph in relation to the dominant image, and which produces words like "crane", "feathering", "down", and "plumaged", and another, over-all movement in which key words, particularly words of sensory significance like "touch", "eyes", and "gazed", are repeated and varied ...

It is important to note that this is something new in literature, and it represents the point, anticipated in Flaubert, at which style ceases to be a relationship between author and reader and becomes a relationship of a magical kind between author and object. Here *le mot juste* is no longer *juste* for the reader, but for the object. It is not an attempt at communicating the experience to the reader, who is supposed to be present only by courtesy, but at equating the prose with the experience. (Ibid, pp. 304–305).

O'Faolain certainly agreed with O'Connor over the relationship between author and reader, and over the limits which must be set on the liberties which may with impunity be taken with language. In an article on Joyce, O'Faolain says :

The truth is that in language Nature and Man have enriched life together. (p. 208).

and later :

Yet it is this continuity – this alltime-spirit as opposed to the time-spirit, the *zeitgeist* – that makes words so rich and overteeming, and here we find the artist declaring that this quality that makes words so rich and full of nuance is exactly the quality that makes of language an imposition that counters his free expression at every step. Thus a man like Joyce would appear to be like an heir who chafes at a will because of the qualifications it contains. But there are qualifications to the whole of the phenomenon of existence and it seems a desperate thing that a man should thus rebel against what is not merely inevitable but inexorable . . . pp. 215–216).

. . . for we must express our thought not so much in words as by means of words. George Moore says the thing well : "In the beginning a language is pure like spring water : it can be drunk from the well – that is to say from popular speech. But as the spring trickles into a rivulet and then into a river it has to be filtered and after long use the language has to be filtered too. The filter is the personal taste of the writer. We call the filter 'style' " . . . Style is the admission of the inadequacy of our materials, it adds humility to art, . . . Style adds a gentle wisdom to art, adds subtlety and suggestiveness and a sophistication that is never weary . . . ("The Cruelty and Beauty of Words", *Virginia Quarterly Review*, 4, [April 1928], p. 221).

Although O'Faolain goes on to condemn Joyce for rejecting the language he has inherited for newer, disjunctive modes of expression, he is still able to adopt or adapt Joycean techniques. For example, there are many passages in the early stories in which words and phrases are repeated either within a paragraph, or within the space of a story. Once again, it will be necessary to refer to a passage from Joyce :

> It had begun to snow again. He watched sleepily the flakes, silver and dark, falling obliquely against the lamplight. The time had come for him to set out on his journey westward. Yes, the newspapers were right : snow was general all over Ireland. It was falling on every part of the dark central plain, on the treeless hills, falling softly upon the Bog of Allen, and, further westward, softly falling into the dark mutinous Shannon waves. It was falling, too, upon every part of the lonely churchyard where Michael Furey lay buried. It lay thickly drifted on the crooked crosses and head-stones, on the spears of the little gate, on the barren thorns. His soul swooned slowly as he heard the snow falling faintly through the universe and faintly falling, like the descent of their last end, upon all the living and the dead. (*Dubliners*, "The Dead", London : Jonathan Cape, 1967, pp. 255–256).

The repetition of words like "snow", "soft", 'fall" has something more than just a mechanical rhythmical effect. It is no longer, in O'Connor's words, a use of "dissociated metaphor". The words do convey associations : associations with death, with the end of the world, with cold, paralysis, emptiness. In addition, the very sound of the sentences in these combinations suggests the meaning of the words. The long syllables, the "s" sounds, evoke the quiet which descends when snow is falling.

Liam O'Flaherty, another Irish writer, appears to have been influenced by this particular passage. In "The Mountain Tavern" the story begins :

> Snow was falling. The bare, flat, fenceless road had long since disappeared. Now the white snow fell continuously on virgin land, all level, all white, all silent, between the surrounding dim peaks of the mountains. Through the falling snow, on every side, squat humps were visible. They were the mountain peaks. And between them, the moorland was as smooth as a ploughed field. And as

silent, oh, as silent as an empty church. Here, the very particles of the air entered the lungs seemingly as big as pebbles and with the sweetness of ripe fruit. An outstretched hand could almost feel the air and the silence. There was absolutely nothing, nothing at all, but falling flakes of white snow, undeflected, falling silently on fallen snow. (*The Mountain Tavern and Other Stories*, Leipzig : Tauchnitz, 1929, p. 91).

Whereas the Joyce passage unites the symbolic with the realistic, switches constantly from what is seen to what is associated with what is seen, from the snow in front of the window to the snow falling all over Ireland, transcends the local to aspire to the universal, O'Flaherty keeps his description – while making use of repetition all through – within the framework of what can be seen, and what can be felt. It is only the snow which is falling. There is no suggestion of "epiphanies". This is not to express a value judgement, but merely to define a difference.

Repetitions of varying kinds are to be found in most of O'Faolain's stories. A highly concentrated use of certain words within one long paragraph will not be found, although words are often repeated within the space of a few sentences. In "Midsummer Night Madness" and "Fugue", one is struck by the constant use of the words "fall", "soft", "dust".

. . . the summer night was falling as gently as dust, falling too on the thousand tiny beacons winking and blinking beneath me to their starry counterparts above. (*MNM*, p. 3).

Fallen hawthorn blossoms splashed with their lime the dust of the road . . . (p. 4).

As I came to a crossways where my road dropped swiftly downhill the tenting chestnuts filled the lanes with darkness as of pitchy night, and under my wheels the lain dust was soft as velvet. (pp. 9–10).

. . . and the doves fluting long and slow in the deep woods through the fallen dark. (p. 17).

. . . a star fell in a graceful, fatal swoop . . . (p. 31).

Here a chill wind was blowing last year's leaves high in the air, but near the lodge where the drive fell sharply down to the gates between the trees on their high ditches the dust lay in soft whispering drifts – soft and white as snow under the moon, so soft that as I stood by the little deserted lodge peering curiously in through one of the windows I might have been a rabbit or a fox . . . (p. 35–36).

There is an owl in the Celtic fable who had seen each rowan as a seed upon a tree, and its length seven times fallen to the earth and seven times over raised in leaf . . . (p. 75).

. . . as if the threshers . . . had blown a storm of cornsheaves against the falling cape of night. (p. 76).

The light fell in a warm glow on the unpainted counter, plain as when its planks first arrived from the town of Macroom twenty miles away and were flung on the kitchen floor . . . The glow fell on the . . . (p. 77).

. . . no bird stirred the wet air : the falling haze made no sound. (p. 86).

In a number of sentences the choice of the word "fall" can only be fortuitous. However, the constant repetition of "fall", "dust" and "soft" might be seen as an extended metaphor running all through "Midsummer Night Madness". On occasions, particularly in the passage in which the narrator feels he becomes part of nature ("I might have been a rabbit or a fox"), the effect, in O'Connor's words, is hypnotic. Here there is no suggestion of symbolic association. O'Faolain goes beyond realistic description, beyond Romantic des-cription. In most of the other descriptions of nature in the story, there has been the suggestion of the bursting-forth of life in nature at this season. Here is the opposite, for no particular reason. Had it been applied to old Henn, the association with dust would have been only too clear. Perhaps in this particular instance, one would have to label the device, extended dissociated metaphor.

On the other hand, there may be some tangible reason for repeti-tive sections in other places. For example in "Fugue" :

So we trudged on and every natural night sound terrified us, a bird's cry, a barking dog with his double note, bark-bark, and then silence, bark-bark, and like that now and again, the whole night long from one mountainside or another. People say the most lonely thing of all is the bark of a dog at night, but to us the most lonely sight was the odd twinkle of a light, miles away, one dot of light and all the rest of the land in darkness, except for the moon in the sky. (*MNM*, p. 66).

This particular passage is one in which the narrator is going over in his own mind what has happened the night before. He is talking to himself. He re-creates it for himself, seeing the countryside, hear-ing the dog, and because he is talking to himself, he repeats to him-self what was repeated out on the mountains. There may also be an attempt – whether conscious or not – to reproduce in prose the kind of conversation which people sometimes have with themselves. Hence the sentence "People say the most lonely sight . . . but to us the most lonely sight . . ." The narrator is not only talking to himself, but creating a second person with whom to talk.

In the same story, there is yet another kind of repetition to be discovered in the first and last paragraphs :

> The clouds lifted slowly from the ridge of the mountains and the dawn-rim appeared red. As I stooped low to peer over the frame of the little attic-window I whispered to Rory that it was pitch-dark; and indeed it was far darker than the night before when we had the full moon in the sky. Rory leaned upon one elbow in bed, and asked me if I could hear anything from beyond the river. ("Fugue", *MNM*, p. 65).

> Down below me in the valley I heard an early cart, the morning wind, light and bitter, sang occasionally in the key of the flooded streams. The dawn moved along the rim of the mountains and as I went down the hill I felt the new day come up around me and felt life begin once more its ancient, ceaseless gyre. (p. 87).

A new day begins in both passages. O'Faolain uses almost the same words to describe the dawn. One day follows the next, inexorably, eternally. Hence the last paragraph ends with the Yeatsian word, "gyre", a further indication of the eternal, unchanging rotation of the seasons. By describing the dawn in both cases with very much the same words, O'Faolain emphasizes this fact, thus bringing the language the writer uses, and what the story is trying to express very close together.

Two further kinds of repetition have still to be noted : deliberate repetition of key-words, or words which are used for descriptive purposes throughout a story, and certain words which are just used frequently in the stories. Mad Henn's neck is referred to all through "Midsummer Night Madness" :

> I can see him running back for his swim, and his long legs and his long neck, that gave him the nickname of "Henn's Neck" cutting through the air as he ran. (*MNM*, p. 6).

> I knew him at once by his long collarless neck . . . (p. 19).

> . . . pulling down his long neck like a snail or a tortoise at the approach of danger. (p. 27).

> . . . and I thought the long neck drew into itself again. (p. 28).

> As their eyes met the swan's neck curved up to her lovingly. (p. 28).

. . . smiling quizzically down on them from his swan's neck. (p. 49).

In "Fugue", the young woman is characterized with words which recur :

. . . bare-footed, her black hair around her, a black cloak on her shoulders . . . (*MNM*, p. 68).

. . . her hand on the crown of her head as if to keep in position the hair brushed and close-combed around her skull like a black velvet cap shining in the firelight. She smiled at me as I entered . . . (p. 68).

. . . raised her head towards me and smiled . . . I saw her smile and it tortured me. (p. 69).

. . . but there was in it the scent and light of flowers and the scent of woman and her soft caresses. (p. 70).

I saw her always as she had come to us in the night, her black cloak hanging heavily against her skin as she led us to the quiet kitchen and the dead embers on the hearth. (p. 74).

. . . and once again I thought of the girl in the black cloak . . . (p. 78).

. . . and turning when I spoke touched her soft hair . . . (p. 81).

. . . she answered, patting her hair with the fingers of her hands : how soft it looked ! (p. 82)

Looking at her soft eyes, and at her soft hair my eyes wandered down to the first shadows of her breasts . . . (p. 85).

Yet everywhere they slept sound abed, my dark woman curling her warm body beneath the bedclothes . . . (p. 86).

In the case of Henn, the repetition serves to establish one physical attribute, whereas with the girl, two impressions are created : one pictorial, the other associative. The pictorial element comes in the simple, repetitive emphasis of black – the suggestion of the death of all human feelings at this time. The blackness of the girl's cloak and hair are in contrast to the description of womanly attributes, conveyed through the repeated adjective "soft".

Certain words are to be found quite regularly in the early stories, particularly certain verbs. There is no apparent reason why they should be used so frequently, since the repetition does not serve any particular purpose. It must be assumed that such regular use is just coincidental. In "Midsummer Night Madness", for example ;

It was a wonderful old house . . . its two gable windows like two cocked ears . . . (*MNM*, p. 7).

. . . He wore a little faded bowler-hat cocked airily on one side of his head . . . (p. 19).

And he cocked his hat still further over on one ear . . . (p. 26)

. . . his old hat cocked forward on eyes that streamed . . . (p. 36).

. . . and so weak did his eyes appear to be that even in the dim filtered light of the station he had cocked his hat forward over his eyebrows . . . (p. 55).

It is true that most of the examples here refer to Henn. Some reason for the repetition might be seen here. However, apart from indicating that he rarely if ever took his hat off, and that when worn, the hat was set at a rakish angle, there is no clear reason for the repetitions.

Other verbs which are to be found regularly in these early stories are : "curl", "flicker", "float", "growl", "roar", "curve", "whirl".

THE PRESENCE OF JOYCE IN THE EARLY STORIES

In his chapter on Joyce, O'Connor quotes a passage from the last pages of *A Portrait of the Artist as a Young Man:*

> Art necessarily divides itself into three forms progressing from one to the next. These forms are : the lyrical form, the form wherein the artist presents his image in immediate relation to himself : the epical form, the form wherein he presents his image in mediate relation to himself and to others : the dramatic form, the form wherein he presents his image in immediate relation to others. (*The Mirror in the Roadway*, p. 307).

O'Connor goes on to explain that all three forms are to be found in the *Portrait*. It is important to bear these three forms in mind in examining the language used by Joyce and O'Faolain. O'Faolain says in the Foreword to the *Finest Stories* that in his romantic twenties he was "drowned" in himself. This would suggest that "he presents his image in immediate relation to himself". To some extent this has already been seen in the presentation of nature, which in both stories is reflected through the narrator. The mood of nature has a direct link with the mood of the narrator.

In *Dubliners*, Joyce adopts the "epical" form, even though many of the stories are written in the first person. In this early work, and also in the *Portrait*, Joyce makes constant use of Romantic language of the kind examined earlier in this study. However there is a difference. Even in a story like "Araby", which describes the emotions of a shy young boy in love, the words Joyce uses have what one might call an icy tenderness; they convey a sense of intellectual detachment. There are passages which express with extreme clarity the boy's feelings, but these are prevented from becoming an emotional outpouring on the part of the author by the insertion of words which, while not being out of place, are academic rather than every-day. They serve to keep the emotional tension down. The beginning of the story sets the mood :

> North Richmond Street, being blind, was a quiet street except at the hour when the Christian Brothers' School set the boys free . . . The other houses of the street, conscious of decent lives within them, gazed at one another with brown imperturbable faces. (*Dubliners*, "Araby", p. 29).

Here is personification, but how different it is from the beginning of "Midsummer Night Madness", with its powerful evocation of the falling of night and the effect on a young man of being surrounded by the almost tangible vigour of summer. The young boy plays in the street. Joyce refers to the "career of our play". The rain doesn't fall, it "impinges upon the earth". In thinking of the girl, the young boy employs words and expressions which cannot be said to be commonplace, quite certainly not if it was the author's intention to unite what the narrator feels with the language used by the narrator to describe his feelings. For example, when the boy dreams of the girl :

> What innumerable follies laid waste my waking and sleeping thoughts after that evening ! I wished to annihilate the tedious intervening days. (Ibid, p. 32).

Later, when he is trying to overcome his impatience :

> I sat staring at the clock for some time and when its ticking began to irritate me, I left the room. I mounted the staircase and gained the upper part of the house. The high cold empty gloomy rooms liberated me . . . (p. 33).

Nothing is permitted to come between what the author feels, and what the narrator says. The text must speak for itself. The adoption of unusual or academic expressions puts a slight barrier between the author and his feelings : it also removes one possible barrier between the text and the reader.

Even the use or non-use of punctuation can be of relevance. For example in "Araby" : "The high cold empty gloomy rooms liberated me". Critics have pointed out that by omitting the commas Joyce immediately catches the reader's attention. He stops at each word. It is suggested that these words, standing by themselves, register in the same way as the impressions would on the mind of the boy. There may be some slight recollection of this in "Midsummer Night Madness" : " 'Good night' she said, and left me in a great empty musty room." (p. 34). Commas are inserted in the later editions.

A more striking parallel in presentation may be found in "Araby" and "Fugue". When the young boy (in "Araby") describes the girl, it is very much in terms of the visual :

> She was waiting for us, her figure defined by the light from the half-opened door. (*Dubliners*, p. 30).
>
> I kept her brown figure always in my eye . . . (p. 30).
>
> She held one of the spikes, bowing her head towards me. The light from the lamp opposite our door caught the white curve of her neck, lit up her hair that rested there and falling, lit up the hand upon the railing. It fell over one side of her dress and caught the white border of a petticoat, just visible as she stood at ease. (p. 32).

In "Fugue", the girl – she is never given a name – is presented in the following way :

> From an upper window she called to us and Rory spoke his name. Used to this sort of thing and pitying us, she came down; bare-footed, her black hair around her, a black cloak on her shoulders not altogether drawn over her pale breast, a candle blown madly by the wind slanting in her hand. (*MNM*, pp. 67–68).
>
> She half knelt before the fire to blow it with a hand-bellows, and as she worked her body formed a single curve, one breast on one knee, and her arms circling the knee while she worked lustily at the bellows. I could see the little wrinkles at each corner of her lips – laughter wrinkles, maybe? (p. 82).

In the Joyce passages, the function of the words is to bring out the details of what the light falls on : "The light from the lamp . . . *caught* the white curve . . ." It is as if he switches a spotlight on the girl, or even tries to use words as a spotlight. The language is unambiguous, with no suggestive, vague, or Romantic words. There is once again repetition ("lit", "fall", "white"). The repetition of

"fall" for example, might be seen as the light moving down the figure
of the girl.

O'Faolain works in very much the same way. The words serve to
describe how the girl appeared to the two men as they stood at the
door. A series of fleeting impressions. In the first passage there is no
time for any deeper impression to be created. In the second, there is
more light. The writer looks at the girl, sees all of her, not just where
the light falls, although again it is the small details which he mentions.

The use of this verbal spotlight (O'Faolain sometimes talks in
terms of "camera angle") can be noticed in several other instances.
In "Fugue", for example :

The light fell in a warm glow on the unpainted counter . . .
The glow fell on the soiled and mutilated bank-notes . . . (*MNM*,
p. 72).

In "Midsummer Night Madness" :

The wind shook the heavy leaves of the chestnuts and as they
scattered benediction on us the light from the little Gothic window
shone on their wet leaves, and on her bosom and chest and knees.
(p. 12).

Only a shaft of wavering light lay thrown across the tiny hallway from another room. Moving cautiously to the other window I
peered in again. There they were, Gypsy and Henn : she with her
skirt drawn above her knees, an old coat over the warm skin of
her bare shoulders, toasting her shins to a little flickering fire . . .
(p. 36).

THE INTEGRATION OF NATURE

Nature in these early stories is often personified, thus becoming
almost a character in its own right. In "Midsummer Night Madness", the narrator on occasion even identifies himself with nature :
". . . as I stood by the little deserted lodge peering curiously in
through one of the windows I might have been a rabbit or a fox . . ."
(*MNM*, p. 36). There is still the feeling that man not only has a link
with the countryside, but that nature possesses powers of purification.
This impression is emphasized through the employment of Romantic
language (the incidence of words like "sweet", "gentle", "soft"). Nor
is it just a general, imprecise idea of nature. Summer is the time at
which nature is at its most prodigal. The descriptions of birds and

plants all add to this sense of the "madness" in which nature is caught up every year. They are not extraneous decoration, irrelevant to the rest of the story. The narrator finds himself almost intoxicated by the forces of nature.

Nature may even be reflected ironically through the condition of the girl. She is pregnant, but her situation is anything but natural. Gammle, the gypsy, appears to be a "child of nature", a creature of unwitting impulse, used by the two knowing men. In any case the rather squalid story in the mad-made house is accompanied and surrounded by nature. Each time the narrator leaves the house, he is once again made aware of a sense of relief. At the end of the story nature even appears to be trying to enter the house.

> Not until late noon did I hear another sound, and then it was the birds singing and the croaking corncrake and the doves in the high woods, and when I rose the whole house was radiant with sunshine reflected from the fields and the trees. (*MNM*, p. 54).

In "Fugue", the narrator does not identify himself with the countryside he passes through. He seems to hate it. "Rory . . . called a curse from Christ on the whore of a river that was holding us here . . ." (*MNM*, p. 65). The narrator does not go out into nature voluntarily, he is forced. The season, although appropriate to the mood of the story, is also against him. Autumn here is not "a season of mists and mellow fruitfulness", it is a time of damp, cold fogs, physical misery. A further change for the worse comes at the end:

> Yet everywhere they slept sound abed, my dark woman curling her warm body beneath the bedclothes, the warmer for the wet fall without, thinking if she turned and heard the dripping eaves – that the winter was at last come. (p. 86).

Altogether nature is used in a much more subtle way in "Fugue". Although the narrator's attitude to nature is negative, it is largely determined by force of circumstances. He does not assume that others automatically are of the same opinion. A contrast is established between how the narrator imagines the girl's future (marriage in the traditional fashion and acceptance of the peasant's lot) and what she says when they meet for the second time. Her dislike of life in the country is not only expressed in the conversation they have but also in the words used. No longer is nature soft, gentle, starry, sweet. The descriptive words become unambiguous, bear no further associations with them: desolate, lonely, bare, high. When the boy protests:

D

She halted in her step and faced me : the little mouth was gathered into a hard white button of flesh.

"You would soon tire of these mountains! The city though, that's where I'd like to live. There's company there, and sport and educated people, and a chance to live whatever life you choose." (p. 83).

The implicit suggestion is that nature and man have gone their separate ways. The boy, presumably coming from the town, finds himself in alien surroundings. The girl wishes to leave the country, which can no longer provide her with what she feels she should have from life. Nature is not a part of the story, but it forms an expressive background to the feelings of the boy and girl. There are references all through to the eternal rhythm of nature ("spool revolving in a shuttle", "the wheel of the passing years"). Even the title, "Fugue", contains within it a suggestion of the mechanical repetition of certain patterns. The story begins with a dawn, and ends with a dawn. As has been seen, the words describing these two mornings, though re-arranged, are more or less the same. Where nature is personified in this story, there is no sense of oneness with the narrator.

Down below me in the valley I heard an early cart, the morning wind, light and bitter, sang occasionally in the key of the flooded streams. The dawn moved along the rim of the mountains and as I went down the hill I felt the new day come up around me and felt life begin once more its ancient, ceaseless gyre. (p. 87).

The wind is personified; it sings in a light and bitter key. The verb carries no associations with it, and has to be qualified.

In "Midsummer Night Madness", verbs often need no further elaboration (for example, "doves fluting in the woods"). It is not important here to point out that both words are clichés. What is important is to establish that in "Fugue", nature is an entity, existing in its own right outside the narrator. In "Midsummer Night Madness" nature often becomes a part of the narrator. However even in "Fugue" there are moments when the narrator is tempted to see in nature something more than just a cold and hostile element. After meeting the girl, his thoughts return to her again and again. Then comes a passage in which the description of nature slowly changes from the tangible to the suggestive. For a moment, the boy almost slips under nature's mantle.

When at last they ceased and our hearts returned to a normal beat we were come to a little lowflung wood of birch and rowan, the silver bark peeling black stripes horizontally from the birch, the red berries of the rowan windblown on its delicate branches. Grey rocks covered the interstices of the trees and the sun fell sometimes on the rock to warm the cold colour : a stream twisted through the rough ground and its sound was soft and bass, and up on a sudden promontory silhouetted against the sky was a single figure who was working in a series of vigorous thrusts on a spade. We remained in the little wood for many hours, listening to the bass-viol of the falling water, to the wind pulling at the larchtops and shaking the tender rowan, and sometimes listening with attention to the drumming of a lorry as it passed in and out of earshot in the near distance.

Excited by danger, and by the beauty of this calm place, the falling stream beside me, the trees moving all around, I began again to think of the young woman in the black coat who had become aware that I too lived ... (*MNM*, p. 74).

In an article on Stephen Crane, W. Gordon Milne explains :

Crane introduced colour primarily to make of his writing a series of lightning images. Believing that a novel 'should be a succession of . . . clear strong, sharply outlined pictures, which pass before the reader like a panorama, leaving each its definite impression', he presented on his page a group of vivid tableaux, painted in strong colours, reds and yellows, grey, black, brown, white, green, blue, purple, orange. ("Stephen Crane : Pioneer in Technique", *Die Neueren Sprachen*, 7, [July 1959], p. 297).

There can be no doubt of the effectiveness of the presentation of a series of substantives qualified by simple adjectives of colour. The impression is, once again, pictorial; there are no associations which the words provoke by themselves. This may not always be the case, as has been seen in the use of the darker colours ("dark", "black") in connection with the girl. At the end of the O'Faolain paragraph, there is also a startling simile which evokes a clear picture in the mind's eye (the little black engine jumping like a kettle on the hob).

THE PRESENTATION OF CHARACTER

Some difference in character-portrayal may be discovered by comparing these two stories. There is a good reason for this difference. O'Faolain would certainly consider "Midsummer Night Madness" to be a tale, and "Fugue" a short story. While there can be no final agreement on where the two forms differ, O'Faolain's own definition is quoted here as a guideline :

As I see it a Short Story, if it is a good story, is like a child's kite, a small wonder, a brief, bright moment. It has its limitations; there are things it can do and cannot do but, if it is good, it moves in the same element as the largest work of art – up there, airborne. The main thing a writer of a short story wants to do is to get it off the ground as quickly as possible, hold it up there, taut and tense, playing it like a fish . . . The limits of the Short Story are apparent. It may not wander far : it has to keep close to its base-point, within the bounds of place, time and character; it will only carry a few characters, three at least, at best not more than three; there is not time, or space, for elaborate characterization – we are flying a kite not a passenger-balloon or an aeroplane; and there is often no plot, nothing much more than a situation, and only just enough of that to release a moment or two of drama, enough to let the wilful kite swirl, change colour, catching the winds of mood. A short story is concentrated stuff . . . A Tale is quite different. Like a small plane it is much more free, carries a bit more cargo, roves farther, has time and space for more complex characterization, more changes of mood, more incidents and scenes, even more plot. Because it is more relaxed the reader may find the Tale easier reading, and he may even take more pleasure in it, but it is likely to give the writer-craftsman rather less pleasure, since what he always most enjoys is the fascination of what is most difficult. (*The Heat of the Sun*, pp. 7–8).

It is therefore reasonable to expect more "elaborate characterization" in "Midsummer Night Madness" than in "Fugue". "Midsummer Night Madness" is built around the character of Henn although it would be incorrect to pretend that the story is only about Henn. He is the centre-point from which everything else radiates. Although he does not know Henn, the narrator relates what he has heard about him. His view is, understandably, one-sided, and reveals as much about himself as it does about Henn.

The introduction is anecdotal, the narrator re-telling stories he has heard from others. He bases his own judgement on these and on his prejudices towards any member of the oppressor class. The narrator soon establishes certain physical details of Henn, particularly the long neck which is referred to all through, largely by means of metaphors and similes :

I knew him at once by his long collarless neck and his stork's legs, and his madman's face beaked and narrow like a hen.
Even here indoors he wore a little faded bowler-hat cocked airily on one side of his head, and over his shoulders and draping his body a rug. He had the face of a bird, mottled and bead-eyed, and

his hair, tawny in streaks with the blister of oil, had one lock at the back that stood out like a cock's comb. (*MNM*, p. 19).

The influence of Joyce again is apparent, as the following passage demonstrates :

> Stephen shook his head and smiled in his rival's flushed and mobile face, beaked like a bird's. He had often thought it strange that Vincent Heron had a bird's face as well as a bird's name. A shock of pale hair lay on the forehead like a ruffled crest : the forehead was narrow and bony and a thin hooked nose stood out between the close prominent eyes which were light and inexpressive. (*Portrait*, p. 78).

For once Joyce is quite open in his enjoyment of puns. The description of the young man is clearly an attempt to demonstrate how similar he is to the bird of the same name. O'Faolain does not explain, but the comparison of a man with a name like Henn with a cock and a hen is rather obvious. In the O'Faolain passage, there is even a change in the normal sentence order :

> . . . and over his shoulders and draping his body a rug.

It would be more usual to place "a rug" at the beginning of that phrase. Joyce often shifts sentences round in this way :

> . . . and touched with the wonder of mortal beauty, her face. (*Portrait*, p. 175).

The impression of the state of degeneracy and decrepitude of Henn and his household is intensified through references to the squalor in which he lives :

> . . . and indeed there was everywhere a musty smell of rooms long abandoned or never tended. His drawing-room was just as I expected, a good room but battered and unkempt like a ragged tramp. At the farther end was a great superfluous fire and standing by it he poured out a jorum of whisky in a glass whose crevices were brown with the encrustations of years, all the time peering at me round the side of a pink-bowled oil-lamp whose crude unshaded light made everything look even more drab and dirty – the bare uncarpeted floor, the fine marble fireplaces mottled and cracked, the china cabinets with broken glass and no china in them; and I remember the look of the yards with their rusted churns and staveless barrels, and everywhere and on everything the fur of mildew and green damp. (*MNM*, p. 21).

In the description of Henn, Stevey and the girl, there is concentration on details which either fit in with other characteristics, or which help to suggest these. In the case of the girl, it is her powerfully physical appearance; with Stevey, his clumsiness, wild hair and slouching shoulders, added to the narrator's statements about his impulsiveness and unreliability. The girl is introduced in the following way :

> She had me by the two arms now, her full bosom almost touching mine, so close to me that I could see the pouches under her eyes, her mouth dragged down wet and sensual, the little angry furrow between her eyebrows . . . the light shone . . . on her bosom and chest and knees. For a second I thought her blue apron drooped over her too rich, too wide hips. (p. 12).

Examined carefully, this passage does not do more than convey a vague impression of the girl, while intimating her physical presence. Questions remain unanswered. Why were there pouches under the girl's eyes? The text does not say. "her mouth dragged down wet and sensual" is cliché. The phrase has no logic. It is suggestive but confusing, whereas "the little angry furrow between her eyebrows" is clear. The light illuminates the girl's figure, although it is not easy to appreciate the difference between "bosom" and "chest". The poetic expression "bosom" might also be criticised. The ironic implications of "too rich, too wide hips" have already been explained.

Later, when Henn and the girl are sitting together, there is a passage which tries very hard to stress the incongruity of the ill-matched pair. It is a good example of what O'Faolain means when he talks about the writer who "luxuriates goes on with the echoes of his first image or idea".

At this stage in the story, both of these characters have already been described more than adequately. As has already been seen, some cuts and alterations were made here in the later edition. In the original there are unnecessary repetitions, and phrases which are cliché or meaningless.

> Strange to watch the unequal pair looking at one another so long, so silently, *seeming not to say one word* to each other, her dark head bowed sidelong to his lips, *her fallen lashes on her cheeks; her parted lips that never moved,* he, with a smile, *foolish yet tender,* sagging his quivering mouth apart, his old hat cocked forward on eyes that streamed their water to his cheeks; and yet, though Henn was *old and decaying,* and she *warm-fleshed, white to her teeth, full of the pride of youth,* and – Henn was right – her

breasts like tulips fully blown, if anything *too magnificently full, too Jewess soft*, yet he could do for all that raise his hand with so much *languid grace* to feel their roundness, hold the *precious globe* for one moment ... (*MNM*, p. 36).

Elsewhere too, phrases and words occur which are examples of "fine effects" ("dancing liquor", "The swan's neck curved up to her", "sniffed a long sneer") or of cliché : "hardened toper", "painted lips", "tilted eyebrows", "tinted London beauty", "the woman, in a massive hat, had flaunted her way to her carriage", "light-o'-love".

Two passages from "Fugue" in which the girl is described are particularly revealing :

> From an upper window she called to us and Rory spoke his name. Used to this sort of thing, and pitying us, she came down; barefooted, her black hair around her, a black coat on her shoulders not altogether drawn over her pale breast, a candle blown madly by the wind slanting in her hand. (*MNM*, pp. 67–68).

> She had put two eggs into a little black pot of boiling water, and the water bubbled and leaped around them with a hissing. A blast of wind came down the chimney and drove a cloud of fire-smoke into the kitchen. We sat silent and presently went to the table and she poured me red tea to drink and I cut the brown loaf and plastered it with butter and jam, and ate greedily. She sat before the fire, ... (p. 83).

What strikes one most in these two passages is not what is said, but what is left unsaid. Nowhere in "Fugue" is the girl clearly described. Not even her name is given. The writer concentrates on presenting two major impressions : the visual and the emotional. The girl stands at the door, with the light falling on her. She is later seen in the house, beside the fire :

> The young woman who had opened the door the night before stood like a statue before the wide fireplace, her bright arm bare to the elbow, and – curious gesture – her hand on the crown of her head as if to keep in position the hair brushed and close-combed around her skull like a black velvet cap shining in the firelight. (p. 68).

It is a verbal sketch in black and white. Even the phrase "her bright arm bare to the elbow" is just another way of adding to the black-and-white effect. The adjectives have been reduced to a minimum. The repetition of certain words has already been mentioned.

The emotional effect is achieved in two ways. After meeting the girl, the boy begins to feel that life perhaps has a "less miser purpose". They have hardly spoken. The girl smiles at him. O'Faolain does not describe the smile; he later comments on the effect.

> She had looked at me as if we had between us some secret love : not one woman in ten thousand will look so at one man in as many thousand ... (p. 70).

In the second passage, something else happens. Even in this early story, O'Faolain employs, to use T. S. Eliot's phrase, the "objective correlative".

> The only way of expressing emotion in the form of art is by finding an "objective correlative"; in other words, a set of objects, a situation, a chain of events which shall be the formula of that *particular* emotion; such that when the external facts, which must terminate in sensory experience, are given, the emotion is immediately evoked. (T. S. Eliot, *The Sacred Wood*, London : Methuen, 1969, p. 100).

The challenge for the writer in this story is to find ways and means of demonstrating what it feels like to live outside society. O'Faolain shows just one or two of the deprivations suffered by such an involuntary outsider : lack of company, lack of love, the sense of being shut out. The boy looks at the workings of society, but has to pass on. He spends a night at one house, the next at another, or out in the open air. He sees the old couple talking, is aware that they will be glad to see him go. He spends an hour with the harvesters; is with them but not of them.

He meets the girl again. O'Faolain describes the preparation of a simple meal. Outside, the storm blows. It is a humdrum every-day scene. For the young man it brings a heightened sense of what he is missing : the comfort of a home and a woman. Later, when they are about to kiss, O'Faolain once more chooses to emphasize the emotional and physical solace that human beings can find in each other's company :

> Smiling at me as a sick woman might smile upon a doctor who brought her ease from pain she slipped my hand beneath her blouse to where I felt the warmth of her skin and her warm protruding nipple, and I leaned to her for a kiss. (p. 85).

In this story, very little information is given about the two main figures. They remain unnamed. It is not known whether they meet again. Very little is told of their appearance, opinions or characters. The narrator describes his feelings all through the story. These change according to the situation in which he finds himself. However even in these extended interior monologues the narrator's thoughts are kept firmly fixed on the effects of being alone. There are no backward looks to his life before, although there are backward looks to almost pre-historical times. The result is that while less is attempted in terms of plot, character-diversity and action, there is a clear gain in the concentration on what is essential. The narrator and the girl he loves are not named. Their situation is universal : their problem, one faced by all lovers at times of war and uncertainty.

Early Stories II

LANGUAGE AND TECHNIQUE

It is inevitable from the very nature of language that choice of words implies choice of attitude, the choice of a certain kind of mental structure within which the object is seen, or to which it is assimilated, or by reference to which it is explained. The nature of language is such that there can be no such thing as a neutral transcription of an object into words. Even if language is used as in a police description of a wanted man, it is still used from a pre-selected point of view – in this case, from the point of view that it is of prime importance to make identification possible. It is for this reason that we should be chary of describing any diction as 'realistic' or 'accurate'. 'Accurate' for what purpose? 'Realistic' according to what view of reality? Sometimes one is tempted to criticize a diction on the grounds that things are 'not really' what the poet says they are – not really feathered tribes, but really birds. But, whilst one expression may be less usual than another, birds are as *really* feathered tribes as they are birds or about a hundred sparrows or ninety-eight examples of *passer domesticus domesticus.* What matters most about any one way of referring to a thing is the implications of one's referring to it in this way in preference to others; the particular way chosen implies a kind of speaker with a kind of purpose or point of view which relates the sparrows/birds/feathered tribes to some system of looking at such objects. Criticism of diction is most likely to be illuminating if it concentrates on the relation between the object and the point of view and promotes sensitivity to the way in which words are used to induce attitudes other than those in which everyday language allows us inertly to rest. It is true that a single word, reverberating against the near-synonyms it has displaced, may imply an attitude – as 'steed' or 'nag' or 'favourite' or 'mount' (whichever is chosen) implies an attitude different from what would be implied by choosing one of the other terms available – and in this respect the single word does not matter. But it matters to its context, which means that ultimately criticism of diction resolves itself into consideration of the interplay of certain words in a certain context; single words bring to the poem a potential power which derives from their usage outside the poem but the power is not set to work until it combines or collides with other potentials brought into the poem by the other words it also uses. (Winifred Nowottny, *The*

Language Poets Use, London : The Athlone Press, 1972, pp. 45–46).

As its title indicates Winifred Nowottny's book is a study of the language used by poets. What she says in the passage quoted is equally applicable to an art form which is nearly as concentrated as that of poetry. Two sentences in the passage are felt to be of particular relevance to the present chapter :

It is inevitable from the very nature of language that the choice of words implies choice of attitude . . .

What matters most about any one way of referring to a thing is the implications of one's referring to it in this way in preference to others . . .

In the first chapter attention was concentrated on language, descriptive devices and possible influences. The short story, and to a lesser extent the tale, represent such a distillation of skills that it could be dangerous to examine them with only one aim in view. It will therefore be necessary to try to see the implications of writing a story in a particular way. For this purpose, one representative story has been chosen from *A Purse of Coppers*, O'Faolain's second volume of stories, to demonstrate his increasing mastery of his art. This is not to suggest that the earlier stories are without merit. However the stories in *Midsummer Night Madness* are so disparate that it would be difficult to select one as being representative. Their length, for example, ranges from the few pages of "Lilliput" to the nearly sixty of "The Small Lady". Many of them remain within the bounds of the classical unities of time, place and action, but generally there is not that sense of control which is found in the second collection.

To facilitate an understanding of O'Faolain's technique a comparison will be made between an early story by Daudet entitled "La Diligence de Beaucaire", and "Admiring the Scenery" by O'Faolain. It is hoped that careful examination of the formal presentation and language in each story will reveal certain similarities while illustrating where the two writers differ in the treatment of their material, and hence also help to show why the stories are written in this particular way. There is no intention here to prove that a connection exists between the two stories, although it is very likely that O'Faolain had read "La Diligence de Beaucaire" (he has a chapter on Daudet in *The Short Story*). The stories have a number of striking common features.

Both stories tell of unhappy individuals (O'Connor's "submerged population"). "Admiring the Scenery" is a character sketch of a man who has suffered. The word "sketch" is purposely adopted here, because many writers feel that it is not possible in the space of a few pages to do more than touch in some few details of character.

> Characterisation is something that can be no more than assumed in a short story. (Sean O'Faolain, *The Short Story*, p. 164).

It becomes clear in the course of the story that there has been a tragedy in the life of Hanafan (one of three named characters in the story), a tragedy from which he has never recovered. The reader is given hints, assumes that Hanafan was crossed in love. At the end, the reader makes the curious discovery that the reason for Hanafan's sadness is never told. O'Faolain adopts the "story within a story" technique in a slightly unusual way. Although the story is about Hanafan, O'Faolain has Hanafan tell his two companions about the eccentricities of the former station-master of a remote country junction while they wait for the train. On the face of it, the station-master's fate is quite irrelevant. It slowly becomes clear that even if the station-master is in no way related to Hanafan, there are parallels in their two lives which are mentioned casually or in asides, and that there is certainly more to the story of the station-master than the fact that Hanafan met him on a night which appears to have affected his whole life. At the beginning Hanafan says :

> "Every man . . . lives out his own imagination of himself. And every imagination must have a background. I'll tell you a queer thing. It's about the station-master in this station a few years back." ("Admiring the Scenery", *Finest Stories*, p. 106).

O'Faolain pursues a quite deliberate policy of evasion all through this story, never actually saying what happened to Hanafan to make him bitter, while at the same time revealing his suffering, possibly following the Chekhov dictum :

> Best of all is it to avoid depicting the hero's state of mind; you ought to try and make it clear from the hero's actions. It is not necessary to portray many characters. The centre of gravity should be in two persons : him and her . . . (*Chekhov Letters*, p. 71).

Hanafan makes only two references which draw attention, either directly or obliquely, to the reason for his sadness. When he begins to tell the story of the station-master, he says :

"I was here with a – a – I was here with a – a friend." (ATS, p. 108).

O'Faolain indicates Hanafan's hesitancy by means of punctuation. The text continues :

In that hesitant second he (the small man) saw at once a piece of Hanafan's secret life revealed, a memory of something known also to the priest; the thought of a dead friend – or perhaps a woman – something or somebody that made the memory of that night so precious to Hanafan that he could not speak of it openly. (ATS, p. 108).

In the context it seems natural that Hanafan should be reticent about what has obviously been a painful experience. Nowhere does O'Faolain become more explicit, even if the reader goes on to assume that Hanafan was there with a woman on the night in question, particularly since later, Hanafan ends his description of the station-master with the words :

"This is a lonely place he lived in," whispered Hanafan. "A lonely life. No children. No wife." (ATS, p. 109).

Hanafan's situation might be described as "the story outside the story", since only the effects on him of his personal tragedy are shown. Perhaps O'Faolain is once again following in Chekhov's footsteps :

But in short stories it is better not to say enough than to say too much . . . (Chekhov Letters, p. 106).

"Admiring the Scenery" could be read as being about the station-master. This would be a perfectly acceptable level at which to approach the story. But there are other levels, and it can only be these at which O'Faolain is aiming. Otherwise the references to Hanafan throughout the story would be quite pointless. Furthermore the end of the story would come at the point at which Hanafan concludes his narration of the miserable existence of the station-master. Instead, while Hanafan is talking about the station-master's loneliness and deprivation of even the comfort of his wife and children, Hanafan is really talking all the time of the fact that he has never married, that he is desperately lonely, and that for him, as for the station-master, the situation is hopeless. Furthermore Hanafan is aware of his situation, whereas the foolish station-master continued to live under the illusion that one day his vocal talents would be recognised. It is this parallel which brings home to the reader the sadness of Hanafan's situation. Hence the situation of the station-master, when set against the background of Hanafan's narration, becomes the "formula of that *particular* emotion", and the story becomes charged with the meaning and emotional effect intended by the author.

Loneliness, sadness, hopelessness are conveyed vicariously through a successfully evasive method of presentation. In a chapter on Hemingway's technique, Carlos Baker is referring to this when he writes :

> It is also evident, however, that early in his career, probably about 1922, he (Hemingway) had evolved an esthetic principle which might be called "the discipline of double perception". The term is not quite exact, since the aim of double perception is ultimately a singleness of vision. This is the kind of vision which everyone experiences when his two eyes, though each sees the same set of objects from slightly disparate angles, work together to produce a unified picture with a sense of depth to it. (*Hemingway: The Writer as Artist*, Princeton: Princeton Univ. Press, 1970, p. 55).

It will be helpful to bear in mind another point raised by Baker when he discusses Hemingway's appreciation and presentation of truth. Baker mentions three stages through which Hemingway went in order to eliminate all that was false.

> Beginning with a standard of performance which rigorously excluded the pathetic fallacy, Hemingway adhered to it with a faith just short of fanatical. He still does. Emotion was of course both permissible and, under proper control, necessary. Excess of emotion, however, was never to be allowed. It could falsify both impression and expression. So many of our habits of seeing and saying take their origin from recollected emotion gone stale. If one could cut loose from these habits, three immediate results might be expected. First, you could see what you really saw rather than what you thought you saw. Second, you could know what you felt rather than "what you were supposed to feel". Third, you could say outright what you really saw and felt instead of setting down a false (and, in the bad sense, a literary) version of it. (Ibid, (p. 60).

From the three stories by O'Faolain which have so far been examined it will already be obvious that he is not only aware of the problems involved in presenting emotion, but that he actively searches for new ways of uncovering and expressing the truth. While he can never go to the extremes of reduction and excision so unswervingly pursued by Hemingway, he can see the danger of too much authorial intrusion, of sentimentalism leading to muddled thinking. Chekhov too was keenly aware of these problems :

> . . . when you try to depict sad or unlucky people, and want to touch the reader's heart, try to be colder – it gives as it were a background against which it stands out in greater relief. (*Chekhov Letters*, p. 97).

The background which O'Faolian chooses is the story of the station-master. The reader learns about Hanafan's private sorrow only by inference. In this way O'Faolain remains "cold" in the Chekhovian sense, without being heartless or artless. This is a method of which Hemingway would certainly have approved, even if he would have gone even further in cutting down. In an interview, Hemingway pointed out that :

> In writing you are limited by what has already been done satisfactorily. I have tried to learn to do something else. First I have tried to eliminate anything unnecessary, to convey experience to the reader so that after he or she has read something it will become a part of his or her experience and seem actually to have happened. This is very hard to do and I've worked at it very hard. (*Hemingway and his Critics*, ed. Carlos Baker, New York : Hill & Wang, 1961, p. 34).

In *Death in the Afternoon* Hemingway again discusses how to present what one sees so that it will be visible to others. He refers to a visit to a novillada. A young bull-fighter was badly gored in the leg. Afterwards Hemingway tried to work out what it was that had most struck him at the time. It suddenly came to him :

> . . . it was the dirtiness of the rented breeches, the dirtiness of his slit underwear and the clean, clean, unbearably clean whiteness of the thigh bone that I had seen, and it was that which was important. (*Death in the Afternoon*, London : Penguin, 1966, p. 23).

Hemingway writes that the bone was "unbearably white". This clear, unadorned depiction of what he sees is Hemingway's truth. It is not necessarily an approach which is considered acceptable by other writers. O'Faolain is not prepared to follow Hemingway's example slavishly, particularly in the use of language.

I cannot help thinking that the factually meticulous realistic style is a step backwards, technically (away from this engrossed alertness) though, in my taste, it is a brutal and spiritless and sluggish weapon at all times. Wherever there is wit, or an imaginative stir of humour or passion, or concentration of feeling or observation, we will find the more suggestive language leaping across deserts of literalness, and we chase after its glittering oasis. (*The Short Story*, p. 233).

Even if O'Faolain is aware that, in Levin's words, the adjective is a "luxury, decorative more often than functional", he cannot bring himself to reduce its application to the introduction of words which do not "describe" but "evaluate". (Here Levin is thinking of typical Hemingway adjectives like "fine", "nice", "good").

O'Faolain does work with exclusion and excision, but far more with suggestion and compression.

Telling never dilates the mind with suggestion as implication does. (*The Short Story*, p. 151).

Of course the Hemingway approach is not just "factually meticulous realistic". It too possesses its own powers of suggestion and implication.

PARALLELS :
"ADMIRING THE SCENERY" AND "LA DILIGENCE DE BEAUCAIRE"

In "La Diligence de Beaucaire" Daudet introduces the traditionally ludicrous figure of the cuckolded husband. He does this explicitly, even if a second reading reveals that the narrative is not as casually straightforward as it first appears. An unusual twist is given when the reader discovers that the husband, a knife-grinder by trade, so loves his wife that he can decide neither to punish nor leave her when she returns – as she invariably does – from her affairs with other men. In this story too there is a man who has suffered. Using different methods, both writers achieve a high degree of objectivity. The word "objectivity" needs qualifying. As Wayne Booth points out in *The Rhetoric of Fiction*, objectivity is just one way for an author to *seem* to make himself both invisible and inaudible. It is quite impossible for a writer to put pen to paper without bringing himself into what he writes, even if, by the most scrupulous elimination of direct or indirect comment, his presence is not immediately apparent. Even disinterested reporting reports something. Every word which appears on the page comes directly from the writer and from nobody else. While a writer may choose to tell a story in an objective manner, he can still indicate to the reader, even by such means, that he is not an undirected speaking camera which observes and broadcasts whatever comes before it without any adjustment or selection. So, in "Admiring the Scenery", while remaining inexplicit, O'Faolain's sympathy for Hanafan becomes increasingly felt.

Daudet uses a first-person narrator, although the narrator is not permitted to make direct comment until the end. He is a stranger to the district – or at least is presented as such – who describes what happens. He occasionally comments, but the comments are of a kind an outsider might be expected to make. His difference from the other passengers on the coach is clearly revealed when the driver refers to him throughout as "Parisien". The narrator appears to be describing what he sees, but there are occasions when comment slips in. For example, when describing the other passengers, the narrator talks of the gamekeeper who has struck a shepherd with a pitchfork and been fined for it. He says :

> On a le sang vif en Camargue. (Alphonse Daudet, "La Diligence de Beaucaire", *Lettres de mon Moulin*, Paris : Fasquille, 1969, p. 15. Hereafter cited as LDB).

This later may be felt to be ironic, oblique comment on the knife-grinder's complete lack of spirit. It may indicate that the narrator knows more about the Camargue than he is prepared to admit. It could also be argued that such remarks, being commonplace, are part and parcel of most people's knowledge. Evidence is later forthcoming that the narrator is deliberately trying to create the impression of his ignorance of the knife-grinder's situation, when the baker makes a remark which causes all the passengers (with the exception of the knife-grinder) to burst out laughing, laughter which the narrator pretends he does not understand :

> Il faut croire qu'il y avait dans cette phrase une intention très comique. (LDB, p. 16).

He must have understood the implications of this remark because it is he after all who is telling the story, not the baker. Similarly, earlier :

> Il parait que le boulanger était d'une paroisse . . . (LDB, p. 15).

again suggesting that the narrator is learning as he sits in the coach, when he obviously knows who the baker is all the time.

E

Generally the narrator adopts a light-hearted, chatty manner which on occasion even permits him to address the reader directly : "... et je vous jure que je ne les retins pas ..." (LDB, p. 18).

O'Faolain has no narrator in "Admiring the Scenery" and he keeps direct comment out of the story. Daudet enters his story. At the end he changes the narrator from being a recorder of events into a person who expresses an opinion.

"Admiring the Scenery" ends with Hanafan sitting in a corner of his compartment in the train, weeping. O'Faolain adds nothing to this. He has set the scene : the reader can go on from there to imagine what he wishes, to draw what conclusions he may. This is not to suggest that O'Faolain has omitted to imply the direction in which the reader's thoughts should go. Daudet goes much further; and destroys his story. It is important to stress that from the very beginning, the impression is that the narrator is being objective, that he is being directed to make the reader feel that the narrator too is experiencing something of whose outcome he has no knowledge. And yet the story is not even told in the present tense. It starts off : "C'*était* le jour de mon arrivée. J'*avais* pris la diligence." The author is aware of what is coming, even if he has the narrator pretend that he does not know the identity of the knife-grinder, or why he is so sad. Throughout the story the narrator maintains the pretence of being uninvolved, even though, as will be seen when the descriptive approach is being examined more closely, it becomes clear that more information is being given than is consciously appreciated by the reader. Towards the end of the story the narrator's attitude suddenly changes. As he gets down from the coach, he looks towards the knife-grinder, who addresses him in the following way :

> "Regardez-moi bien, l'ami, me dit-il d'une voix sourde, et si un de ces jours vous apprenez qu'il y a eu un malheur à Beaucaire, vous pourrez dire que vous connaissez celui qui a fait le coup." C'était une figure éteinte et triste, avec de petits yeux fanés. Il y avait des larmes dans ces yeux, mais dans cette voix il y avait de la haine. La haine, c'est la colère des faibles ! . . . Si j'étais rémouleuse, je me méfierais. (LDB, pp. 19–20).

This concluding section has a two-fold effect. It suddenly reveals the knife-grinder as a fool and a buffoon, while introducing a melodramatic tone for which there is not the slightest need. More important still, it suggests that the knife-grinder does not love his wife at all, that he is consumed by impotent anger and hatred, whereas from what the other characters in the story have stated, he is supposed still to be in love with his wife.

". . . C'est que chaque fois c'est la même comédie. La femme part, le mari pleure; elle revient, il se console." (LDB, p. 18).

All along the implication is that the husband has been so hope-lessly in love with his beautiful wife that he is prepared to forgive her everything. There has been an implicit sympathy running through the story too, since the outsider (the narrator) records what the local people feel. The narrator shows how amused the peasants are at the lack of "manliness" demonstrated by the husband, the suggestion being that the baker, for example, would soon have shown who was the master in the house. By remaining outside the local framework, merely reflecting what he sees, the narrator has never-theless managed to insinuate that he feels sorry for the knife-grinder. Sometimes this impression has been strengthened by asides : "le pauvre rémouleur", "le pauvre homme". At the end, Daudet sud-denly makes his narrator come out with a statement of astonishing banality : "La haine, c'est la colère des faibles", which completely destroys his credibility. The narrator comes even further into the story with the final remark, which is presumably intended to illus-trate the humour of the situation : "Si j'étais rémouleuse je me méfierais.". The contrast in method of the two writers is perhaps most strongly demonstrated by this ending, since both have adopted – almost word for word – the same way of showing the chagrin of their main characters. "Admiring the Scenery" ends thus :

Tired and sleepy, nobody noticed that, in his corner, Hánafan was weeping to himself, the drops creeping through his tightly closed eyes. (ATS, p. 111).

In one of the concluding paragraphs of "La Diligence de Beau-caire" the narrator says :

Ni lui non plus, le pauvre homme ! Il ne dormait pas. De derrière je voyais ses grosses épaules frissonner, et sa main – , une longue main bafarde et bête, – trembler sur le dos de la banquette, comme une main de vieux. Il pleurait. (LDB, p. 19).

The first passage marks the end of the story : the second merely marks the beginning of the end. The comments which follow it have already been quoted. O'Faolain would certainly argue that the Daudet ending tries to do too much. What is more, and worse, through his narrator Daudet destroys his main character with the concluding remarks. This is not to suggest that the statement "La haine, c'est la colère des faibles" is incorrect, but merely that it is completely inappropraite in this story. Such authorial intrusion – through the medium of the narrator – leads to loss of control in an emotional situation, and hence to a break in logical and aesthetic consistency. In his chapter on Daudet, O'Faolain quotes Henry James :

> Daudet is nothing if not demonstrative; he is always in a state of feeling; he has not a very definite ideal of reserve. (*The Short Story*, p. 54).

and Conrad, who is even more dismissive :

> His characters' fate is poignant; it is intensely interesting; and not of the slightest consequence. (Ibid, p. 55).

CONCENTRATION : FRAMEWORK

Both of these stories are short : they achieve succinctness and compression in various ways. They take up little time : "Admiring the Scenery" only the interval between waiting for and entering a train; "La Diligence de Beaucaire" the period taken to travel some distance by coach in the Camargue. But within this compass more is revealed than just a narration of what occurs within these miniature time-frames.

Hanafan relates what has happened in the past. The reader sees the effects on him of these past events at two removes : firstly in time, secondly through the fact that the tragedy which alters Hanafan's life and character irrevocably is never revealed.

The Daudet story comes at one remove, since it is the baker who tells the narrator the details of the knife-grinder's unhappy marriage. The main events here too lie in the past. Nothing new happens in the story, except that the reader learns who and what the knife-grinder is. Concentration is also attained in this, as in many stories, by the use of place. In "Admiring the Scenery", it is the station platform, later the train carriage; in "La Diligence de Beaucaire", the inside of a coach. Place can also incorporate environment. Intimate knowledge of a district or country – for example O'Faolain's association with Ireland and his native Cork, or Daudet's with the South of France – can also make for concentration of a slightly different kind : the presentation of the universal from within the local. A small world, but a complete one, and a world in which what occurs may be understood in terms of a much wider stage. There can be no suggestion that these remarks apply solely to the short story. It is nevertheless interesting to note that many of the recognised masters of the short story start from what they best know : where they grew up. Joyce, Maupassant, Faulkner, immediately spring to mind.

As far as the telling of the stories is concerned, O'Faolain and Daudet waste few words on an introduction, although they do introduce their stories. It has become a normal feature of the modern short story for the writer to come right into the centre of events at the beginning. In these two stories there is a little limbering-up before things start to happen – if one is even justified in talking of "happenings" in stories in which the narration is largely of things past.

O'Faolain appears to make a leisurely start. Daudet is more direct : "C'était le jour de mon arrivée ici." Daudet goes on to describe the carriage and his five travelling-companions. This he does in the space of two paragraphs.

O'Faolain begins with a description of an evening in early spring. The seasonal background at first sight appears to have no great relevance to the rest of the story. Later, this reference to the re-awakening of life in nature can be regarded as being in ironic contrast to the life-denying existence of the priest, the arid, testy personality of the little man, and to the dead hopes of Hanafan. In the second paragraph O'Faolain briefly adds details of these three figures:

> The three men . . . They were waiting for the last train to take them to the country town where they all three taught in the diocese college. (ATS, p. 103).

Each of them is then described fully. O'Faolain takes the external appearance of the priest as a basis for comments on his character. To a more limited extent he does the same for the other two men although with them, he gives no more than hints as to character. Daudet does more or less the same, although once again there is a further interesting parallel. In both stories, the main character is left until last, and in both instances, the writer appears to go out of his way to intimate that this particular character is not important. In "Admiring the Scenery", Hanafan at first is not even named. He is just called "the third man". The next paragraph begins :

> There was nothing remarkable about this third man . . . (ATS, p. 104).

although the sentence continues :

> . . . except that he had handlebar moustaches and a long black coat and a black hat that came down low over his forehead and shaded his melancholy face . . . (ATS, p. 104).

The striking point is that although the author is introducing his main character, he keeps him till last and deliberately says that there is nothing remarkable about him.

Daudet is even more sparing of details. He presents a lumpish shape under a huge rabbit-skin cap. Both authors hide their main characters under hats. O'Faolain goes on to describe Hanafan's features in some detail. Daudet's knife-grinder is introduced with the words :

> Enfin, sur le devant, près d'un conducteur, un homme . . . non ! une casquette, une énorme casquette en peau de lapin, qui ne disait grand-chose et regardait la route d'un air triste. (LDB, p. 14).

What he is and who he is are revealed much later. Certain adjectives accompany both figures through the story. Hanafan's face is described as "melancholy". On the same page there is the phrase "the sad Hanafan", on the next, "looking sadly at the warmth of the sun . . .". A sudden change occurs when Hanafan goes on to talk about that one decisive evening in his life. He is no longer sad.

> The teacher said these words, strength, sweetness, richness, with a luscious curl of his thin lips . . . his eyes widened . . . a small glow on each cheek. (ATS, p. 107).

> His eyes dilated under his black hat with the image of this memory. His eyes were not cranky now, but soft and big. (ATS, p. 108).

Towards the end, as the remembrance fades :

> His eyes had become cranky and tormented again. (ATS, p. 110).

The Daudet story contains similar passages. For example :

> . . . et se tournant vers la malheureuse casquette, silencieuse et triste dans son coin . . . (LDB, p. 16).
> . . . le malheureux leva brusquement la tête, et, plantant son regard dans le mien . . . (LDB, p. 19).

At this stage of the discussion, it is only necessary that attention should be drawn to such key words as "black", "sad", "cranky", "triste", "malheureux". Here they are to be seen more in the context of technique than of language. It is of course important to ask why these words and not others are chosen. This will be done later. But it is equally important to look at these words as having the function of evoking a characteristic feature of the person so described which establishes that characteristic in the mind – not so much in the mind's eye. Hanafan is sad, the knife-grinder is "malheureux et triste". These words, accompanying the characters through the story, constantly nudge the reader, remind him – even if it is no longer necessary – of that one aspect of his character on which the writer is choosing to concentrate.

NATURE

O'Faolain introduces nature, both in his description of Hanafan and as a backdrop to the story. This is not true of "La Diligence de Beaucaire". Elsewhere (for example, "Les Etoiles") nature is very present. Examination of "Fugue" and "Midsummer Night Madness" showed that nature was not a fortuitous element. Nor is it here. The setting in "Admiring the Scenery" is a spring evening. The three men at the station stand against this background. For all three the sight of nature has either lost its relevance (the priest), become a matter for mere intellectual questioning (the small man), or provokes feelings of sorrow and loss (Hanafan). The three men are not described as looking at the green things of nature, or even listening to the sounds of spring birdsong introduced in the first paragraph. They lean (like old men) against the uncomfortable rail and look towards the sun – which is setting. They are men for whom the elemental things in life have died. The priest is resigned :

. . . a man who had gone through many struggles and finally solved his problems in a spirit of good-humored regret. (ATS, p. 103).

Hanafan, remembering what happened on this very platform, despairs, is reduced to tears at the end. The third man's problems are never stated at all, but everything he says or does, suggests aggressiveness, frustration and bitterness. Looked at in the light of the stories in the first collection, there is a change to be noted. Although they come from a country in which one is never very far from nature, none of the men has any direct contact with nature. This may well be why they just talk about it. For them nature is to be thought of only in intellectual or metaphysical, but not physical terms.

The small man refers his companions to "our gardener at home" :

". . . he'd be lying of a hot summer's afternoon under an apple tree – a lazy old ruffian – 'Grand day, Murphy,' I'd say. 'Oh, a grand day, God bless it,' he'd say, 'and isn't it good to be alive?' But that's not admiring the scenery," went on the small man. "It's not being *conscious* of it. It isn't, if you understand me, projecting the idea of the beauty of the scene, the idea, into one's own consciousness. Is it now, Hanafan?" (ATS, p. 105).

This is quite a departure from what was found in the two stories from the first collection. The narrator in "Midsummer Night Madness" did project himself into nature.

A change was apparent in "Fugue", although there was still powerful personification of nature. A conscious break with an attitude became perceptible, a break which is perhaps being referred to in the remarks about the old gardener. He is still part of a dying, if not already defunct, attitude to nature. Generally speaking, nature is seen from the outside, from a distance, sometimes, as in "A Broken World", from behind glass (inside the train compartment). The three men in "Admiring the Scenery" live in the town, belong to an urban civilisation. This is a community which has passed, or is in the process of passing, the stage at which nature can be seen as offering spiritual balm. Nature is a phenomenon which can be reflected on and discussed in intellectual terms, but which, even for Hanafan, does not register in the way it does for the narrator in "Midsummer Night Madness". He does not come back from his walk in the country refreshed. Hanafan is "dog-tired". This fact of man's increasing alienation from nature must be kept in mind when later stories are being analysed. If nature, in a Romantic sense, is dead, then using it in the traditional way, to imply emotional states or situations, may no longer be permissible, or can only be done at the danger of applying something which is extinct to suggest something which is alive.

Daudet's stories, written at a much earlier period, are set in an area which was largely agricultural in its structure and where the contact between man and his surroundings was still close. It therefore comes as no surprise to find Daudet using a nature-setting for his story into which his characters fit with ease and where they are quite unconscious of further associations. Nature is all around, is still lived with.

REPETITION

The appearance of the same, or similar, descriptive adjectives for the two main characters in both stories has already been referred to. Certain phrases, expressed by characters in both stories, by the fact that they are repeated, reflect on those who use them, becoming almost a refrain to accompany the main themes. For example in "Admiring the Scenery", Governey is constantly heard saying, "What a country". This phrase works as a two-way reflector in that it shows up his personal intolerance, and is also a comment on Ireland, which generally in this collection of stories, is not seen in very favourable light. O'Faolain makes more frequent and varied use of repetition than Daudet – as has already been seen in "Fugue" and "Midsummer Night Madness". In the Daudet story, one phrase occurs again and again. When, making fun of the knife-grinder, the baker refers to the knife-grinder's wife, the unfortunate man keeps on saying, "Oh ! tais-toi, boulanger, je t'en prie . . .". Towards the end, even the narrator picks this up :

> J'avais toujours dans les oreilles ce "Tais-toi, je t'en prie," si navrant et si doux . . . (LDB, p. 19).

The comment by the narrator is helpful, for it states quite explicitly the effect of such repetition – "navrant et doux". These are spoken repetitions. There are others of a different kind in both stories. Governey is always the "small man". At the beginning he is introduced as "a small, dark man, with a slim small body and a button of a head . . ." (ATS, p. 104).

In the descriptions of nature it is also possible to see a certain consistency in the words chosen. There is the change from hopeful nature in spring, to cold nature in winter, to the dark unpleasant night. This can only be deliberate. In every case, the words describing the season or nature, are mood-forming. There is also a striking contrast between the various descriptive terms, from key words like "black" (used both of nature and in the regular description of Hanafan) to more Romantic words like "rich", "deep rich", "deep". The romantic expressions have a more direct emotional effect, since they are linked with an emotional situation and thus gain significance which does not come from their meaning, but from the fact that because they are inserted in unusual contexts, the reader is forced to think about them, to decide what such terms can signify ("rich night", "deep", "rich night", "A lovely, thick night"). This is not to suggest that other expressions which are unambiguous cannot work beyond their surface meaning. For example, terms used to suggest the less pleasant moods of nature – the mountains becoming "black and cold" – may in addition imply the reality of Hanafan's lonely, empty life.

When the sun goes down behind the mountains, all colour immediately disappears from the side where there is no more light. What could be more normal? The chill is immediately felt when the sun stops shining at this time of the year. A casual reading of the story would not make the reader feel there was anything unusual in such descriptive terms. However, there is not much space for description in a short story. Every phrase, every word, must fit, must have its place. One is therefore justified in asking why, for example, the sunset is introduced at all. Having done that, and having read the story through, one can begin to realise why such adjectives as "black" and "cold" are chosen. This impression is strengthened when the same adjectives appear again and again, sometimes in slightly different combinations. For example, when the men get into the train, those in the compartment have a "cold and damp look" (ATS, p. 110). In the last paragraph, once more : "Then the three friends were left alone in the cold, damp carriage" (ATS, p. 111).

"Moon", a word which has strong romantic associations, also appears on a number of occasions. Twice Hanafan refers to the title of a song, a favourite of the station-master's, "The Moon Hath Raised Her Lamp Above". The night which so affected Hanafan's life was "one hard, moonlight night in December".

> "Well, one hard, moonlight night in December, I was here, like this, waiting for the last train back to Newtown. The snow was white on the hills. It was blazing. There wasn't a sound but the wind in the telegraph wires. The clouds were in flitters, in bits. I well remember it. A rich night. A deep, rich night, and no harm in the winds, but they puffing and blowing." (ATS, pp. 107–108).

Here one finds a combination of the two kinds of language so far discussed. Although the night was "hard", it was also "rich". This may have been unwitting on the part of the writer, but judging by what has so far emerged from looking at this story, it seems unlikely. This mixture is most clearly revealed in the fact that although the night was "hard" (frosty) it also becomes "rich". This change in the kind of language might be explained through the significance of the night for Hanafan. The impression created in the story is that at least during the time Hanafan was at the station he was with some-

body who not only meant a great deal to him but who presumably
felt for him an equally strong attachment. Thus although tragedy
comes after this night and is associated with it, when put into words,
Hanafan's recollections are naturally marked by this contrast. This
is perhaps a most striking example of what Winifred Nowottny means
when she says :

> What matters most about any one way of referring to a thing
> is the implications of one's referring to it in this way in preference
> to others; the particular way chosen implies a kind of purpose or
> speaker with a kind of purpose or point of view . . . (*The Language
> Poets Use*, pp. 45–46).

Returning now to the repetition of the word "moon", one can
find : "the white moon in the mountains", and later, as Hanafan and
his anonymous companion leave the station in the train, "We saw
the moon in the flags of the Liffey . . ." (ATS, p. 110).

One is tempted here to make further deductions about the significance of the fact that the moon is seen in reflection, and not in
the sky. First the moon as a symbol of love; now just a painful
reminder of something which has ended.

The influence of George Moore was mentioned in the first chapter,
particularly in connection with the collection of short stories entitled
The Untilled Field. Hans Kast has this to say of Moore's use of
repetition :

> George Moore läßt nach Art des Leitmotivs bei Wagner zur
> Verdeutlichung eines bestimmten Gedankens oder Gefühls immer
> wieder analoge Sätze auftauchen . . . Gleiche Worte, analoge
> Sätze, wiederkehrende emotionale Beschreibungen bilden die
> stilistischen Kennzeichen dieser sorgfältig angeordneten Gesch-
> ichte. (*George Moore und Frankreich*, Diss., Tübingen, 1962, p.
> 112).

As far as "Admiring the Scenery" is concerned, it is largely the
repetition of descriptive words or phrases, and individual substantives
which catch the attention. In addition to "moon", the words "lamp",
and in particular "lonely" recur. Loneliness is not only a theme in
many of the stories in this collection – either explicit or implicit – the
word itself occurs again and again. "A Broken World" for example
begins : " 'That's a lonely place !' said the priest suddenly." However neither in this story nor in later ones does O'Faolain take repetition to the extremes found in Moore and Joyce.

There is a passage in "Admiring the Scenery" which might well be
traced back to "Home Sickness".

Every man . . . lives out his own imagination of himself. And every imagination must have a background. (ATS, p. 106).

At the end of "Home Sickness" when James Bryden, an old man now, thinks of his return to Ireland when he so nearly married an Irish girl, Moore suddenly says :

There is an unchanging, silent life within every man that none knows but himself, and his unchanging, silent life was his memory of Margaret Dirken. The bar-room was forgotten and all that concerned it and the things he saw most clearly were the green hillside, and the bog lake and the rushes about it, and the greater lake in the distance, and behind it the blue line of wandering hills. (*Modern Irish Short Stories*, ed. Frank O'Connor, London : Oxford Univ. Press, 1957, p. 16).

O'Faolain, taking over from where Moore (and others) had left off, does not work in quite the same way. Moore not only makes the statement that every man has within him "a silent, unchanging life", he goes on to make this quite explicit by describing what this means in terms of James Bryden, who, while passing the autumn of his life in exile, in his heart still remains bound to his native soil, and to the girl he left behind.

O'Faolain aims at creating the same impression, but avoids such direct commentary. In "Admiring the Scenery", it is Hanafan who makes the statement quoted, but he does so in the course of a conversation when it might easily seem to be of no more than general application. It comes early on, long before the reader is even aware that Hanafan is the main figure. In the Moore story, the passage comes as summing-up and comment in the last paragraph. It is important to point out that Moore refers to Margaret Dirken by name, but says nothing more of her. What he does describe ("the things he (James Bryden) saw most clearly") are the details of the countryside. These, Bryden can visualise clearly. He goes on to describe them, using adjectives. In that re-created landscape which has been preserved in his mind down the years, there is no longer a visible Margaret Dirken, merely the feelings of inextinguishable sadness which are evoked immediately his mind goes back to that time. Here too, not necessarily a parallel, but a similarity may be seen in the way that Hanafan talks about the past. Nothing is said about the tragedy, but Hanafan's memory works with astonishing accuracy when he talks about the kind of night it was. That has remained eternally fresh, and creates for him, as for the reader, an immediate sense of sadness. The reader can discover that even though O'Faolain is not prepared to say what the tragedy in Hanafan's life was, somewhere in the story there is a remark which in simple, direct terms, gives the key.

Similar general statements can be found tucked away in many of the stories, although they are not always to be taken at face value. A writer who works in such subtle ways is quite capable of playing tricks on the reader, and of slipping statements into the text which he may be lulled into accepting, not realising that they are ironic. For example, in "The Old Master", the unidentified narrator early on says of John Aloysius Gonzaga Sullivan :

> God alone knows if ever he said to himself in the silence of the night, "John Aloysius Gonzaga Sullivan, you're a sham !" Such men have no life but their own drama, and if you had dared say that to him he would probably have replied, "Is it not as good a life as another?" (*FS*, p. 84).

The story ends :

> . . . but nobody ever thought of him as anything but a free, public show while he was alive, and we only begin to think of him as a human being when he was gone.
>
> I wonder is there any wrong or right in that? Or is it, as John would have said, that one kind of life is just the same as another in the end? (*FS*, p. 92).

THE PRESENTATION OF CHARACTER

At the beginning of the chapter, O'Faolain was quoted as suggesting that character-portrayal is not possible in the short story. This is a statement which he later modifies :

> There is no time or space inside a short story for complex characterization. But, if the situation is an eloquent one, we can, somehow or other, induce a whole personality out of the tiniest incidents within that situation, much as we can see a whole panorama, see the highest mountain in the world, through a tiny pinhole in a sheet of paper. (*Short Stories*, ed. Sean O'Faolain, Boston : Little, Brown and Company, 1961, p. 16).

The three men in "Admiring the Scenery" are described in some detail.

> The priest stood in the middle, a young man, too fat for his

years, with drooping lids, puffed lips, and a red face as if he suffered from blood pressure. The same features on another man might have suggested a sensual nature, but there was in his heavily lidded eyes a look that was sometimes whimsical and sometimes sad, and that look, with the gentle turn to his mouth when he smiled, gave him the appearance of a man who had gone through many struggles and finally solved his problems in a spirit of good-humored regret. (ATS, p. 103).

There are no unusual words, no startling figures of speech, no references to dress. O'Faolain goes from the visible to the invisible. What the writer sees are all details which a casual observer might be expected to notice. Nor, as in "Midsummer Night Madness" for example, is he quite so absolute in his assumptions. He does not say that the priest *was* resigned, merely that his look "gave him the appearance" of someone who had opted out of life. This impression is heightened as the story continues, partly by repetition of the image of the heavily lidded eyes, finally, at the end by means of comparison: "The priest's lidded eyes were as immovable as an owl's." As with Henn, one physical feature is referred to all through, once again with character implications. Whereas in describing the gypsy girl in "Midsummer Night Madness", O'Faolain says that her "mouth dragged down wet and sensual", here, such suggestive statements are modified. "The same features on another man might have suggested a sensual nature". Nevertheless it still remains doubtful if such descriptive terms are really effective since they evaluate what cannot be proven.

Certain aspects of the priest's character are introduced by what he says, or what others say. When Hanafan tells the story of the station-master, he talks of the man's lonely life, of the fact that his wife was dead and his children gone away. A daughter is mentioned. The priest interrupts to say that he was responsible for sending her abroad, apparently not concerned that she had gone to her death. "I sent her there . . . A nice poor girl she was, God rest her."

In discussing priests in stories by O'Faolain, Catherine Murphy finds a curious parallel between their corpulence and their indifference to the suffering of those around them (she quotes as examples, "Admiring the Scenery", "Discord" and "The Man Who Invented Sin"). She goes on to say :

Despite the gentler portrait, however, he (the priest in "Jenny the Wren") shares in the deficiency of human qualities characteristic of the other clerical figures and ascribable to the effects of their commitment to a religious vision : awareness of human suffering without compassionate action; resignation, which the reader is not led to share, to the ills of the world; and an apparently compensatory interest in food and drink . . . (*The Imaginative Vision and Story Art in Three Irish Writers*, Diss. Dublin, 1967, p. 55).

Catherine Murphy's judgment is based on the evidence of several stories. In "Admiring the Scenery" there is only very limited justification for making such assertions. Nevertheless, in addition to the indications already mentioned, there is the fact that the priest finds the story of Boyhan (the station master) amusing, and he makes no comment on several occasions in the story where one might have expected sympathetic reaction. Governey is seen through his appearance which is only briefly referred to ("small dark man, with a slim small body and a button of a head and clipped dark moustaches"). Otherwise he reveals himself through his aggressive remarks and brusque movements. Nothing is known about his past : only a few inconclusive deductions can be made about him from what he does and says. He does not appear to be very pleasant, although even that cannot be said with certainty since so little is known about him. Such terse description is more characteristic of modern short stories than the lengthier introduction of the priest. As the story continues, the priest's resignation and Governey's apparent bitter aggressiveness are indicated by action, or lack of it.

> The main thing about him was that he did break occasionally into sudden talk, and when he did he banged the hard railings repeatedly or lifted his two fists in the air and slapped his forehead. (ATS, p. 104).
> . . . shouted the little man, hammering the railing, (p. 104).
> . . . demanded the small man, leaping backward and whirling his head left, right, and up in the air, as if the answer were a bird. p. 105).
> . . . interrupted the small man, and he wagged his finger into the priest's face. (p. 105).
> The small man's eyes pounced on him . . . (p. 108).
> . . . probed the small man inquisitively . . . (p. 108).
> . . . prodded the small man . . . (p. 108).
> . . . cried the small man, thumping his knee . . . (p. 110).
> . . . the small man kept looking around him restlessly . . . (p. 111).
> The priest nodded, never taking his eyes from the stream or his pipe from his little mouth. (p. 104).
> The priest nodded. (p. 105).

The priest nodded and chuckled aloud. (p. 106).

He (Governey) glanced at the priest, but he had lowered his face and his mouth was clamped. (p. 108).

The priest rose up and knocked out the ashes of his pipe. (p. 109).

The priest leaned back and gave a merry little laugh. (p. 110).

The priest looked at him, and kept looking at him as he swayed with the carriage, but he said nothing. (p. 110).

The priest was still looking at him, so he nodded towards Hanafan and winked. The priest's lidded eyes were as immovable as an owl's. (pp. 110–111).

Taken out of context, the repeated noddings of the priest appear to have no great significance. Reference back to the text will show that on almost every occasion the priest has either just been asked something by Governey which he refuses to answer, or makes no comment on what Hanafan says where one could have expected a reaction.

The presentation of Hanafan, who is described last, is much more complicated. It starts long before he is mentioned, in ways which the reader cannot suspect.

Nothing is really learned about his character. The story is designed to bring out the emotional hurt and despair. Everything serves that one end : the season of the year, the descriptions of nature, the comments or non-comments of the other figures, the story of Boyhan, and Hanafan's actions and words. But how is Hanafan described?

There was nothing remarkable about this third man except that he had handlebar moustaches and a long black coat and a black hat that came low over his forehead and shaded his melancholy face; when he spoke, however, his face was gentle as the fluting of a dove. There was nothing resigned about him; his oblong face was blackberry-coloured where he shaved and delicate as a woman's where he did not. His eyes were lined with a myriad of fine wrinkles. They were cranky, tormented eyes, and his mouth was thin and cold and hard. (ATS, p. 104).

The first sentence may best be understood in the light of O'Faolain's misleading the reader, deliberately playing down the fact that here is the most important figure. Quite apart from what emerges from the rest of the story, even the physical appearance is anything but nondescript. A man dressed in black from head to foot, with his hat pulled down over his eyes, is certainly not unremarkable.

Even later, when Hanafan is telling the story, O'Faolain continues to play his little game. The text reads :

> His eyes widened. Clearly he was seeing nothing but the old station master. (ATS, p. 107).

This just isn't true. Or rather, it is only true in the sense that the writer is attempting to work towards the pain in the heart of this man. He chooses not to do it directly, and must, abiding by the rules of his art, do so here by not telling the cause of Hanafan's broken life.

Once again, as in the description of the priest, the writer goes from the physical to the personal. In the case of Hanafan he does no more than hint at a mystery (the reason for melancholy) although he is definite in the difference he makes between the priest's resignation, and Hanafan's continuing lack of it. In context, there seems to be nothing remarkable about that statement. It is just one of the little pieces in the puzzle, which, as examination shows, fits neatly into its appointed place.

The description of Hanafan is not flawless. It demonstrates most clearly a problem of language which O'Faolain never quite overcomes. However aware he is of the need for ruthless self-discipline on the part of the short-story writer, he himself confesses : "For all I know I may still be a besotted romantic" (Foreword, *Finest Stories*, xi). In this passage there is a rather uneasy mixture of the unambiguous and the Romantic, resulting in loss of control. Up to the first semi-colon, the reader watches as the verbal spotlight passes over Hanafan. Then comes the phrase : "When he spoke, however, his face was gentle as the fluting of a dove". The doves fluted in the woods surrounding Henn's house in "Midsummer Night Madness". Even there, the words "dove" for pigeon, and "flute" for coo, were felt to be Romantic cliché. Here the simile is used not to describe sound, but the expression on Hanafan's face. It is true the phrase is preceded by "when he spoke, however, his face was gentle as the fluting of a dove". Presumably O'Faolain just wishes to imply that when he spoke, the expression on Hanafan's face changed. As the sentence stands, there is the strained application of a metaphor of sound to a person's appearance, attempted by the use of a cliché. The effect is not improved by the continued use of the metaphor.

> . . . his words were like prize pigeons that he released one by one from his hands. (ATS, p. 105).
> . . . went on Hanafan in his downy voice. (p. 105).

F

particularly since the metaphor immediately afterwards becomes mixed :

> Hanafan . . . in his round, womanly voice. (ATS, p. 105).

In the passage in which Hanafan is first introduced, the text continues : "his oblong face was blackberry-coloured where he had shaved and delicate as a woman's where he did not". There can be no objection to the descriptive terms used in this sentence. It is possible to visualise what O'Faolain here presents. But why does O'Faolain go into further detail? There is no obvious answer. It is possible that Hanafan's sensitivity is being referred to in some roundabout way, although this can be nothing more than conjecture. Perhaps it is merely what O'Faolain calls a "fine effect" :

> Of themselves, however, they are no more than virtuosity. If a Fine Effect is not functional it is still a Fine Effect, and worth appreciation, but it will be a Still Finer Effect if it is part of a whole effect, which in the short story means a whole effect in human relationships. (*Short Stories*, p. 24).

If one continues for a moment to go on thinking visually, one might be inclined to feel that omission of that sentence would make the passage (and the figure of Hanafan) clearer. The eyes are important, since they are, like the mouth, referred to all through the story. It is noteworthy that they are first not described, but only mentioned. The reader's attention is drawn to the wrinkles around them. Why? Wrinkles could signify age. Here they are obviously an indication of the despair which has written itself into Hanafan's features. The eyes are important, the wrinkles an essential indirect adjunct in that they say something about the appearance of the eyes, and also about Hanafan. The last sentence contains five adjectives of varying kind and function :

> They were cranky, tormented eyes, and his mouth was thin and cold and hard.

O'Faolain picks up the implication of the wrinkles to come out with a definite statement about Hanafan's eyes. These are adjectives which evaluate. They do not describe in the way that words like "blue" or "large" would. The same must be said of "cold" and "hard". These two adjectives recur all through, and must be considered key words. In the passage there is perhaps an echo of the repeated use of "and" to be found in Moore and Joyce. The para-

graph ends with "and his mouth was thin and cold and hard".
In *Portrait of an Artist* there are passages in which Joyce appears to
be almost revelling in the use of this conjunction.

> Eileen had long white hands. One evening when she was playing
> tig she had put hands over his eyes : long and white and thin and
> cold and soft. That was ivory : a cold white thing. (*Portrait*, p. 37).

This particular passage is bursting with association ("ivory", "cold
nature", sensory impressions). The insertion of the series of "ands"
is presumably to mark the five different impressions on the mind
when Eileen puts her hands over Stephen's eyes, impressions which
range from the visual to the tactile. It is debatable whether the four
"ands" do anything for the adjectives. There is even a danger that
attention could be taken from the adjectives and transferred to
the conjunctions. In the O'Faolain phrase there is not even much
obvious difference in meaning between "cold" and "hard". All that
is achieved, is a slight sense of rhythm. The appearance of "ands"
must not be overstressed, since, although long sentences are to be
found in the story, they are not often deliberately held together by a
series of conjunctions.

This is again a moment at which to bear in mind what O'Faolain
has to say about Joyce, about what writers have learned from Joyce
and how even Joyce's style in places has dated.

> When space presses, language speaks shorthand. The short story
> makes this demand insistently, and readers, over the last fifty years,
> have come more and more insistently to demand it of writers.
> Readers are spry and knowing nowadays and do not like to be told
> things of which they can guess quite well, thank you. From this
> point of view of language Maupassant seems old-fashioned today.
> So does Chekhov, if the English translations do justice to his
> Russian. It is a measure of the speed of this latter-day intensifica-
> tion of language that we can already read much of the earliest
> Joyce with a shock of surprise at the innocence of their style and
> the superficiality (in the literal sense of surface-ness) of their
> English. He tells us things delicately but explicitly :—

> 'Night after night I had passed the house (it was vacation
> time) and studied the lighted squares of window : and night
> after night I had found it lighted in the same way, faintly and
> evenly. If he was dead, I thought, I would see the reflection of
> candles on the darkened blind for I knew that two candles
> must be set at the head of a corpse . . .'

(*The Short Story*, pp. 224–225).

O'Faolain is quite right to find the passage lacking in compression. The visual quality on the other hand is undeniable. The two-way flow from this deceptively simple paragraph (two-way, because it combines a look at the outside of the house, with a simultaneous sense of looking into the boy's mind) is very effective. O'Faolain continues :

> When we read *Dubliners* long ago (first published in 1914) we had a different sensation. We admired the intensity, as we then thought, of the struggle to grapple with the shapes and faces of things, the vivid graphic quality of the descriptive detail. Today there is little of this kind of pleasure in his descriptions. They do not, we observe, grapple to compress, they peer and catalogue painstakingly, and the words are not always well-chosen :—
>
> > 'Ignatius Gallaher took off his hat and displayed a large closely-cropped head. His face was heavy, pale and clean-shaven. His eyes, which were of a bluish slate colour, relieved his unhealthy pallor and shone out plainly above the vivid orange tie he wore. Between these rival features the lips appeared very long and shapeless and colourless. He bent his head and felt with two sympathetic fingers the thin hair at the crown . . .'
>
> Is it true that Ignatius Gallaher 'displayed' his head? That word implies that he wished to show his baldness. 'His eyes . . . relieved his unhealthy pallor', 'Rival features'. Is a tie a feature? The later Joyce must sometimes have smiled at this ingenuous English.
>
> In the same volume we can find a comparison which shows both how language can be dilated or extended, and a foretaste of how Joyce would do it. Re-read the famous conclusion with an eye not on the meaning but on the choice of words which convey it :—
>
> > 'He watched sleepily the flakes, silver and dark, falling obliquely against the lamplight. The time had come for him to set out on his journey westward. Yes, the newspapers were right : snow was general all over Ireland. It was falling on every part of the dark central plain, on the treeless hills, falling softly upon the Bog of Allen and, farther westward, softly falling into the dark mutinous Shannon waves . . .'
>
> (Ibid, pp. 225–226).

This particular passage has already been quoted in an earlier section. It was necessary to re-quote since O'Faolain uses it to demonstrate Joyce's progress in bending language to meanings beyond the simple visual. O'Faolain continues :

Knowing, now, Joyce's sensitiveness to the ultimate vibrations of words we might read too much subtlety into the passage; yet, even if we pretend to know nothing of the compression of the style of *Ulysses*, we may feel that the word 'obliquely' has a more than visual connotation (I mean that the word could suggest perversity and something of obliquity), though the pictorial value of the oblique angle is, I agree, paramount and excellent. We admire the risk successfully taken with the fine adjective 'mutinous waves'; for Joyce's danger, as the story alone would show, always was to be 'literary'. ('His soul had approached that region where dwell the vast hosts of the dead'. Soul . . . approached . . . region . . . where dwell . . . vast hosts. All bookish words; though breathed on.) We admire the lilt, another magnificently successful risk, which enlarges the value of words. (Ibid, p. 226).

In his comments on the Igatius Gallagher passage, O'Faolain draws attention to the inaccuracies and strained metaphors. It is revealing now to return to the description of Hanafan, to see what happens if some phrases are cut from it.

There was nothing remarkable about this third man except that he had handlebar moustaches and a long black coat and a black hat that came down low on his forehead and shaded his melancholy face; when he spoke, however, his face was gentle. There was nothing resigned about him. His eyes were cranky, tormented eyes, and his mouth was thin and cold and hard.

The removal of "Romantic distractors" helps to keep the lines clear. The description is no longer leisurely. The sentences are shorter, the details come in quick succession. Nevertheless they come in a way which makes it possible for the reader to assimilate the information easily, to build up a mental picture based on some few simple unambiguous descriptive phrases and on the deductions which follow from these. All of which enables him to form his own personal view of Hanafan. Admittedly, there is no space for the reader to relax since each word is important. It might be felt that this, by contracting the spotlight, draws too much attention to the visual, whereas he insertion of distractors – whether consciously done or not – can lull the reader into a state of reading along, rather than into, the text. As his critical essays demonstrate, O'Faolain is constantly thinking about how to describe, and about the problems involved in finding a means of combining compression with implication :

Realistic detail, in short, is a bore if it merely gives us an idle verisimilitude : its function is to be part of this general revelation by suggestion. It is fruitful realism when external reality releases the imagination : it is a barren realism when a reader says, 'I could almost see that tree; or smell that pond.' Why should anybody want *almost* to see a tree or smell a pond when he can go out in the field and see a real tree and smell a real pond? Nowhere so much as in a short story are such irrelevant descriptions out of place; there is no time for them : however striking they may be they are among the many things which have to be dropped in this general struggle to make a tiny part do for the whole. (*The Short Story*, p. 163).

Later :

I began by saying that language in the short story has, in our time, become much more alert or engrossed, and I set out to illustrate what I mean. I cannot help thinking that the factually meticulous realistic style is a step backward technically . . . though, in my taste, it is a brutal and spiritless and sluggish weapon at all times. Wherever there is wit, or an imaginative stir of humour or passion, or concentration of feeling or observation, we will find the more suggestive language leaping across deserts of literalness, and we chase after it to its glittering oasis. (Ibid, p. 233).

And yet, while he can criticise Hemingway, O'Faolain readily acknowledges Hemingway's achievements :

. . . I have . . . chosen to put the Hemingway story toward the beginning of the list to illustrate the pleasure which I call the Recognition of the Familiar, because most readers think of Hemingway as a "realist" and therefore immediately and easily extract from his work this sturdy pleasure of Recognition; whereas, in fact, I regard Hemingway as one of the most imaginative writers of our time who merely employs the old realistic technique as a sort of reassuring envelope in which he conveys to us highly disturbing, personal viewpoints of a thoroughly irrational nature . . .

. . . and Hemingway *could* finely illustrate the pleasure which I call the Imaginative Flight were it not that his realistic (or pseudo-realistic) technique conceals his imaginative content as his hairy chest hides his tender heart. (*Short Stories*, p. 2).

In the first of these quotations O'Faolain condemns irrelevant descriptions. In the case of "Admiring the Scenery", one might ask why the story begins in such a relaxed manner, with facetious references to birds. Considered in the light of Hanafan's tragic situation, it seems out of place. In a story which has been seen to contain so much subtly hidden comment and irony, such a beginning can hardly be coincidental. It is obviously ironical, a built-in reflection on Hanafan before his first appearance. Spring has come round again, but it will pass these three by. Only Hanafan is able to take himself back in time to that one decisive night. When he does so, not only do his face and manner change, but the language he uses changes accordingly. Altogether, one of the striking qualities of this story is the dilation gained through implication within the frame of vocabulary which is frequently repeated and deliberately limited. This can best be seen in the descriptions of Hanafan's face and of nature.

From between the little wayside platforms the railway shot two shining arrows off into the vast bogland where they vanished over a rise that might have been imperceptible without them. It was just before sunset in early spring, a soft evening of evaporating moisture and tentative bird song; for the birds seemed to be practicing rather than singing, twirling and stopping, and twirling and stopping, and when the bold thrush rolled out a whirl of sound he might have been mocking all the other eager, stupid little fellows, like the bullfinch or the tits, who had not yet learned their songs. (ATS, p. 103).

... shaded his melancholy face ... His eyes were lined with a myriad of fine wrinkles. They were cranky, tormented eyes, and his mouth was thin and cold and hard. (p. 104).

... said the sad man, Hanafan ... (p. 104).

Hanafan ... in his round, womanly voice, all the time looking sadly at the warmth of the sun fading from the distant grains of snow, and the mountains becoming black and cold ... (p. 105).

... and leaves the world to darkness and to me ... (p. 105).

... and the way the fields were all gentle and dark and quiet ... (p. 105).

The teacher said these words, strength, sweetness, richness, with a luscious curl of his thin lips around the fruit of sound. His eyes widened. Clearly he was seeing nothing but the old station-master. Earnestly he went on, a small glow on each cheek. (p. 107).

Again Hanafan's cold lips sucked the sound of those words, rich, deep, and his eyes dilated under his black hat with the image of his memory. His eyes were not cranky now, but soft and big. (p. 108).

When they climbed into a carriage the windows were speckled with rain and the three men inside, who leaned back to let them pass, had a cold, damp look. (p. 110).

... Hanafan, whose eyes had become cranky and tormented once more. (p. 110).

Then the three friends were left alone in the cold, damp carriage, listening to the battering rain. (p. 111).

In the slow, deceptively light-hearted opening to the story, there is no obvious indication that the writer is aiming at compression. The descriptive words are precise in the first sentence, become less so as the paragraph continues : ("soft evening", "twirling", "whirl of sound", "bold thrush"). It is also noticeable that Hanafan in his "slow" voice is restrained in his vocabulary. Only when he starts to talk about that one night do his appearance and language undergo a sudden transformation. The words he speaks are words which have been encountered in the earlier stories – words of Romantic origin. It is interesting to note that O'Faolain not only comments on what the teacher says, but he himself for a few phrases, slips into the same style. Here too, one wonders if judicious pruning would not have improved these sections. For example :

> The teacher said these words, strength, sweetness, richness, *with a luscious curl* of his thin lips *around the fruit of sound*. His eyes widened. Clearly he was seeing nothing but the old station master. Earnestly he went on with a small glow on each cheek : (ATS, p. 107).
> Again Hanafan's cold lips *sucked the sound of those words rich, deep*, and his eyes dilated under his black hat with the image of his memory. His eyes were not cranky now, but soft and big. (p. 108).

By referring again to the words which Hanafan employs, and doing so by means of dubious metaphor, O'Faolain adds nothing to the effect. Indeed there is a distinct danger that he waves with a flag when his intention is to give the gentlest of nudges. How very much more effective, for example, are the two verbs "widen" and "dilate". Hanafan's eyes widen, the reader sees into and beyond them. It is in such touches that the story begins to leap.

For much of the story, the language used to describe nature is kept within the bounds of the simple visual. There are exceptions : for example, at the beginning where there may well be a deliberate attempt, if not to mislead, at least not to spoil the ultimate effect by introducing it too soon.

There appear to be interesting gradations in emotional level, from words like "sweet", "rich", "deep", which carry with them associations of past joy; down through "gentle", "dark", and "quiet" which, taken in connection with the quotation from the "Elegy" and with the fact that "gentle" is found both in the description of the priest and of Hanafan, convey almost a sense of suspended animation. One slowly discovers the cunning way in which nature is employed all through as a mood reflector.

As the story becomes increasingly sad – a word which recurs in one form or another throughout – there come repetitions of "black", "cold", "damp". Nature is not generally personified, it is more often introduced with the intention of suggesting the brittleness of a mood : for example, "the warmth of the sun fading from the distant grains of snow, and the mountains becoming black and cold". Although the words "black" and "cold" have meanings which are perfectly clear from the context, they may still work at another level in that they are to be found in the first description of Hanafan, and come to be associated with him as the story proceeds. So that here, while being applied to nature, it is not a personified nature, but just the appearance of nature which is being employed as a mood-reflector. Furthermore, even apparently simple words may be seen to have their own radiations.

The adjectives are not unusual or cliché. They are part of common usage, although they have not been so hard-worked as to have become meaningless, nor are they used in such a way as to become meaningless. In adopting adjectives like "fine", "nice", or "good", for example, Hemingway evaluates what he sees, without influencing the reader.

The repetitions have the effect of helping the adjectives in "Admiring the Scenery" to go on working at various levels, since they are not always applied to the object which they are intended to qualify. Their importance is emphasized through the subtle ways in which they influence the story – for example, through nature and the weather.

Once again quotations from literature are inserted to intensify the mood which the author is trying to create. The passages are apposite to what is happening at a particular stage of the story and since Hanafan is a literate man they do not seem out of place. The question still remains whether they are essential. All that can be said of this story is that for those who know the "Elegy Written in a Country Churchyard", the poem will have associations. For those who do not the significance will be lost.

Another writer will be called in to sum up a chapter in which O'Faolain's maturing skills have been seen at work in a story, which, while not flawless, in its quiet way radiates, dilates, takes the reader along that rare path which leads to the "ultimate vibrations".

The first necessity for the short story, at the set out, is *necessari-*

ness. The story, that is to say, must spring from an impression or perception pressing enough, acute enough, to have made the writer write. Execution must be voluntary and careful, but conception should have been involuntary, a vital fortuity. The sought-about-for subject gives the story a dead kernel, however skilfully words may have been applied : the language, being *voulu,* remains inorganic. Contrived, unspontaneous feeling makes for unquickened prose. The story should have the valid central emotion and inner spontaneity of the lyric; it should magnetize the imagination and give pleasure – of however disturbing, painful or complex a kind. The story should be as composed, in the plastic sense, and as visual as a picture. It must have tautness and clearness; it must contain no passage not aesthetically relevant to the whole. The *necessary* subject dictates its own relevance. However plain or lively or unpretentious be the manner of the story, the central emotion – emotion however remotely involved or hinted at – should be austere, major. The subject must have implicit dignity. If in the writer half-conscious awe of his own subject be lacking, the story becomes flooded with falseness, mawkishness, whimsicality or some ulterior spite. The plot, whether or not it be ingenious or remarkable, for however short a way it is to be pursued, ought to raise some issue, so that it may continue in the mind. The art of the short story permits a break at what in the novel would be the crux of the plot : the short story, free from the *longueurs* of the novel is also exempt from the novel's conclusiveness – too often forced and false : it may thus more nearly than the novel approach aesthetic and moral truth. It can, while remaining rightly prosaic and circumstantial, give scene, action, event, character a poetic new actuality. It must have had, to the writer, moments of unfamiliarity, where it imposed itself. (Elizabeth Bowen, *Collected Impressions*, London : Longmans, Green, 1950, pp. 42–43).

Later Stories I

MATURITY AND MEDIACY

In the later work O'Faolain is clearly on his own. The influence of other writers, in particular of Joyce and Moore, has been shrugged off. There is a definite move away from the intense, occasionally mannered techniques found in some of the first stories.

Altogether an increasing sense of relaxation is conveyed in two main ways : through the method of presentation, and through the words O'Faolain uses. The rather literary style of many of the early stories gives way to a much more informal manner. Although he often draws on the other arts, O'Faolain now less frequently brings in allusions to painting or music in the struggle to stress or add depth to what he writes. This does not mean that the reader is being written down to, or that the writer is being any less fastidious in his choice of vocabulary. O'Faolain merely turns his back on earlier models, to be free to express himself in the superficially simpler language of every day. Through this he breaks one link between himself and what he writes – at least for the reader – because the reader will not be tempted to think that there is one language for literature and another for him, thus automatically, unconsciously accepting that what is written comes directly from the writer, represents the way he sees things. Simple diction clears the mind, while metaphor may dazzle or bemuse.

In his analysis of Hemingway's technique and style, H. E. Bates has something rather similar to say :

> What Hemingway went for was that direct pictorial contact between eye and object, between object and reader. To get it he cut out a whole forest of verbosity. He got back to clean fundamental growth. He trimmed off explanation, discussion, even comment; he hacked off all metaphorical floweriness; he pruned off the dead, sacred clichés; until finally, through the sparse trained words, there was a view. (*The Modern Short Story*, Boston : The Writer, Inc., 1968, p. 169).

The later O'Faolain stories are seldom directly subjective, even if there is often a first-person narrator. The writer, or the narration, is merely the medium through which events are passed on to the reader. A deliberate attempt appears to have been made to work in mediate, rather than in immediate, terms. Joyce explains this process towards the end of *Portrait* :

> The narrative is no longer personal. The personality of the artist passes into the narrator itself, flowing round and round the persons like a vital sea. This progress you will see easily in that old English ballad "Turpin Hero" which begins in the first person and ends in the third person. . . . The personality of the artist, at first a cry or a cadence or a mood and then a fluid and lambent narrative, finally refines itself out of existence, impersonalises itself so to speak. (p. 219).

O'Faolain is never able to "impersonalise" himself totally to reach that final stage demanded of the writer by Joyce. O'Faolain appears to be convinced that the second stage is as much as can be expected, indeed even desired, so that while the subjective may be diminished, there remains that distilled sense of what he calls "communicated personality".

O'Faolain continues to tell stories. Much still remains beneath the surface, but Joycean "epiphanies" are rarely found (a striking exception being "The Silence of the Valley").

As in the earlier work, O'Faolain often writes round a central idea which is sometimes tucked away in the text. In the two stories to be examined in this chapter, these ideas are the relationship of pity to love ("Up the Bare Stairs"), and of pride to humility ("Lady Lucifer").

A difference in the handling of the material becomes noticeable. Whereas in such stories as "Admiring the Scenery" and "The Old Master", O'Faolain also works from a central statement (in "Admiring the Scenery" it is "Every man lives out his own imagination of himself"; in "The Old Master", "such men have no life but their own drama") the characters representing these statements are never permitted to go beyond living out their own limitations. They are men whose existences remain stunted and blighted. It is the difference between being asked to feel with a Hanafan ("Admiring the Scenery") about whom and about whose previous life one learns little, and with the doctor in "Lady Lucifer" who has faced up to the problems of life and mastered them. This is not to suggest that the writer has an obligation to present only characters who have come to terms with themselves and with the world around them, but rather that the method successfully employed in "Admiring the Scenery" is not one which is always to be applied. Certainly it imposes limits on what a writer can and cannot do, limits which he may feel to be intolerable. It might possibly be argued that this is one of the distinctions between the short story and the tale, although reference to shorter pieces in the later collections would show that even in these O'Faolain tends to reveal more, enabling him to go deeper.

In "Up the Bare Stairs" for example, a younger O'Faolain might well have introduced Nugent in quite another way. Instead of permitting Nugent to tell what happened in chronological fashion, leaving out nothing essential, O'Faolain would probably have had Nugent talk all round this one crucial event in his life. He might have described his professional career, he might have mentioned the parents without discussing what they did to him; he might have referred to the teacher-priest, without so clearly describing the effect Angelo had on him. He does none of these things.

Whereas in "Admiring the Scenery" one sees only the marks which unexplained sorrow have burned into Hanafan's features, in "Up the Bare Stairs" one is told what lies behind the lines on Nugent's face.

Further ease of manner comes in the person of the narrator; through this, an awareness of the presence, or lack of it, of the writer. No writer, in spite of what Joyce advocates, can absent himself completely. At best a seeming absence will be attained. In a story like "Dividends" the narrator is even named. But calling the narrator, Sean, does not necessarily mean that the reader will consider the identity of the narrator to be of great importance, or that what the narrator feels and says, is what the story is about. The Sean of "Dividends" is an older, worldly-wise narrator who casts a knowing, mocking eye on what passes before him. He is no longer the passionate, impressionable, named narrator of "Midsummer Night Madness" whose changing, changeable viewpoint so powerfully influences the direction in which the reader's thoughts are bent. Generally, the "I" figure of the later stories sees, hears, speaks, without being as directly involved as he is in stories like "Fugue" or "Midsummer Night Madness". Even where the narrator is not immediately concerned, as for example in "A Broken World", he is still drawn to take a more active part through some issue which is introduced in the course of the story, or through strong feelings which are aroused at what is said to him. The narrator in "A Broken World" cannot just listen passively to the priest and country farmer he meets on the train. He has a point of view of his own which is expressed; he is part of a triangular situation. The narrator in "Up the Bare Stairs" remains disinterested. It is possible that he is, or stands for, Sean O'Faolain. This would not make any difference to an appreciation of the story. The narrator listens while a perfect stranger tells him the story of his life. The two men have certain formative experiences in common – their home town of Cork and the school which both attended. These two facts are coincidental and merely, after the conversation has started, provoke Nugent to tell the story of his life. The very structure of the story tends to support this assertion. The narrator does not speak once while Nugent tells of his early life. He comes in at the beginning to introduce the story, and at the end to round it off. He expresses an opinion, it is true, but it is the response one could expect of a person who is hearing something for the first time. In "A Broken World" the narrator constantly argues with the other two men, interrupting and commenting all the way through. He is drawn into a discussion in which he is forced to take sides. The narrator in "Up the Bare Stairs" stresses that Nugent's story does not touch his own life :

> Then he leaned forward and let down all his reserves. As he began my heart sank. It was the favourite theme of every successful man. 'How I Began.' But as he went on I felt mean and rebuked. I doubt if he had ever told anyone and before he finished I could only guess why he chose to tell me now. (UTBS, *The Man Who Invented Sin*, p. 144).

At the beginning of the other story the narrator first describes the priest as "a bloody bore", but then finds himself ever more deeply embroiled in an altercation over Ireland.

Where an opinion is expressed in the later stories it is often done in such an urbane, self-deprecatory manner as to suggest that the narrator's judgement is as fallible as anybody else's. This may be seen as a natural development from attitudes noticed in the first stories. Even there, even in a story like "Midsummer Night Madness", the impetuous young narrator finds that his harsh, one-sided, rigidly defended attitudes, if not changed, become modified as he looks at the other two men : the youthful, hopelessly irresponsible revolutionary, and the old man, representative of a dying landowner class.

At the same time, comment, criticism, or condemnation may emerge from under the later urbanity. For all the light-heartedness of "The Man Who Invented Sin", the narrator does speak his mind to condemn narrow-mindedness, and to express his sadness at those who refuse or who are unable to be honest with themselves. But even where he censures (for example when he is shocked that Majellan should later in life feel that the innocent fun he and the other monk, Virgilius, had had in the company of two nuns while attending a course on Gaelic, had been wrong) O'Faolain can still

show understanding for the vagaries of human behaviour. The monk
admits :

> 'You mightn't understand it, now! But it's not good to take
> people out of their rut. I didn't enjoy that summer.' I said I under-
> stood that. After a few more words, we parted. He smiled, said he
> was delighted to see I was looking so well, and went off, stooping
> his way back to his monastery in the slum. (*The Man Who Inven-
> ted Sin*, p. 17).

Thus in the later stories a rather different impression is left with
the reader, both where there is a narrator and where another narrative method is adopted; the impression of a writer who knows where
he stands, who is concerned, but who is no longer acting out his own
fate through his writing, no longer identifying personally with the
characters he creates. As a mature artist O'Faolain stands back, permitting his characters to make or unmake mistakes, being aware of
man's eternal unpredictability. He would no doubt agree with
Somerset Maugham :

> I think what has chiefly struck me in human beings is their lack
> of consistency. I have never seen people all of a piece. It has
> amazed me that the most incongruous traits should exist in the
> same person and for all that yield a plausible harmony. (*The
> Summing Up*, p. 40).

In his study on Sean O'Faolain, Maurice Harmon discusses this
realisation of the opposing forces at work within the individual :

> The appearance of "Lady Lucifer" (1941) shows O'Faolain
> working out a rationale. In the course of this story the whole prob-
> lem raised in *Purse of Coppers* is discussed. The alternative solu-
> tions are traditional : exile to a more adventurous and competi-
> tive existence where one can realize one's self to the fullest extent,
> or retirement within the hermitage of an accepted insufficiency.
> The chief character is a specialist in mental diseases, a rational,
> scientific Irishman, who has travelled much outside the country.
> Like many characters in *Purse of Coppers* he is a man of divided
> loyalties – emotionally and atavistically drawn to the country of
> his birth, imaginatively and intellectually attracted to the wider
> world outside. His defence of that attraction contrasts with his
> enjoyment of the quiet, rural setting in which the story takes place.
> Men of ambition, he argues, need a full life; man's pride in him-
> self demands it. The Irish, he says, have too much humility and
> therein lies the cause of their failure. His argument contains fami-
> liar references to loss, damnation, and inner disunity :

Pride and humility aren't opposites. They're two sides of the
same thing . . . If a man is born proud he must feed his pride. It
was something given to him. Once he starts the humility tack
he's lost. Lost and damned. Drowned in the opposite of his own
pride. Show me your humble man and I'll show you the pride
coiled up in his humility devouring it like a worm. Show me
your proud man and I'll show you the humility flowering
beneath his pride like a crocus under the snow . . .

The significant point about the doctor's defence is that it enables
him to face up to his divided state successfully. He is the first to
move beyond the condition of loss. He does so by an acceptance of
human nature as inherently composed of opposing forces. Like the
priest in "A Broken World" he is concerned with the "composi-
tum" of one's being, the full life. For both, anything that denies
the achievement of a full personality is harmful, mentally and
spiritually. But whereas the priest was defeated by his knowledge
of evil, the doctor was not. His positive stance is based on a sane
and healthy point of view. "All our emotions," he says, "are a
tension of opposites. It depends from hour to hour which way the
balance swings." (Maurice Harmon, *Sean O'Faolain: A Critical
Introduction*, London : University of Notre Dame Press, 1966,
pp. 94–95).

Ireland and the Irish remain the subjects of the stories, even
where the action is placed abroad. O'Faolain continues to look for
what is universal in the tiny world of Ireland, so that while the men
and women who people his work are seen in Irish surroundings, the
reader comes to realise how eternally similar are the problems of
man even when the outer circumstances are disguised by local
customs, local colour.

More or less exclusive recourse to a certain milieu however can
bring with it problems of a special kind : for example, that what is
generally believed to be "typically Irish" may come to be used in
the same way. There is a difference, a very important difference,
between the bachelor main character in "Unholy Living and Half
Dying" who is recognisably, but not exclusively, Irish, and Benjy
Spillane ("Childybawn"), a man who is so tied to his mother that
he can only marry when he is nearly fifty, after his mother has died.
Whereas Cardew's problem is one which can be seen within a much
larger framework (loneliness, ageing, death), Benjy Spillane, his
mother, and the girl he finally marries, are held in the strait-jacket
of a situation which is seen as "typical", hopeless, amusing. Little
attempt is made to go beyond surface recording, the reader being
asked to laugh at a situation whose implications are potentially
tragic.

Increasingly O'Faolain writes about city dwellers whose contact with nature is minimal. Even in the early work most of the characters were no longer part of a pastoral tradition whose influence was still perceptible, but dying. Nevertheless in "Midsummer Night Madness" the presence of nature was not only felt, but became a living, associative entity. The narrator on occasion was one with nature. Later, O'Faolain cannot just turn his back on what lies beyond the city boundaries. Here too, a change both in attitude towards and description of nature will be found. Sometimes this even takes the form of an expressed indifference. At the beginning of "Up the Bare Stairs", the narrator says of Nugent :

> After a casual interest in the countryside as we left Kingsbridge he had wrapped a rug about his legs, settled into his corner and dozed. (UTBS, p. 141).

These later stories are fixed firmly in the present. Only occasionally are there references back. Earlier there was often a sense of the past still living on (e.g. "Fugue", "A Broken World"). Such links become more and more tenuous, and in a story like "The Silence of the Valley", are seen to have been irrevocably broken.

So far O'Faolain's work has been examined chronologically. There is no implication in this that maturity is necessarily to be equated with greater excellence. The lasting worth of many of the early stories remains undisputed. As Graham Greene said in his review of *A Purse of Coppers:*

> "The Old Master", "Sinners", "Admiring the Scenery", all have the same superb grasp, the fist closed simultaneously on the particular character, his environment and the general moral background of the human mind failing always to live up to its own beliefs . . . One salutes, in these stories, an immense creative humour, as broad in speech as Joyce's gloom. (*The Spectator,* 3.12.1937).

Two stories, "Lady Lucifer" and "Up the Bare Stairs", have been chosen for particular attention in this chapter. Both have technical and contentual features which have been met with in earlier stories :

> Third-person narrative.
> Three friends going out into the country.
> One of them telling a story.
> Discussion of nature, revealing attitudes to it.
> Story within a story.
> ("Lady Lucifer", "Admiring the Scenery").

First person narrative.
Meeting on a train.
Encounter with a stranger.
Story of crucial incident in stranger's life.
("A Broken World", "Midsummer Night Madness", "Fugue",
"Up the Bare Stairs").

THE PRESENTATION OF CHARACTER

She had me by the two arms now, her full bosom almost touching
mine, so close to me that I could see the pouches under her eyes,
her mouth dragged down wet and sensual, the little angry furrow
between her eyebrows. The wind shook the heavy leaves of the
chestnuts and as they scattered benediction on us the light from
the little Gothic window shone on these wet leaves, and on her
bosom and chest and knees. For a second I thought her blue apron
drooped over her too rich, too wide hips. Since I did not speak
she shook me like a dog and growled at me as fiercely as a dog.
("Midsummer Night Madness", *FS*, p. 7).

There was nothing remarkable about this third man except that
he had handlebar moustaches and a long black coat and a black
hat that came down low on his forehead and shaded his melancholy
face; when he spoke, however, his face was gentle as the fluting
of a dove. There was nothing resigned about him; his oblong face
was blackberry-colored where he shaved and delicate as a woman's
where he did not. His eyes were lined with a myriad of fine
wrinkles. They were cranky tormented eyes, and his mouth was
thin and cold and hard. ("Admiring the Scenery", *FS*, p. 104).

The doctor was poling. He wore brief cream bathing-trunks : a
finely-built, sandy-haired man, serious but not severe. He had
studied in Vienna, New York, and London; he was a specialist in
mental diseases; he was just back from six years with the British
Army in the East; he bore himself with the authority of experience
and power. ("Lady Lucifer", *The Man Who Invented Sin*, p.
121).

All the way from Dublin my travelling companion had not
spoken a dozen words. After a casual interest in the countryside
as we left Kingsbridge he had wrapped a rug about his legs, settled
in his corner and dozed.

He was a bull-shouldered man, about sixty, with coarse, sallow
skin stippled with pores, furrowed by deep lines on either side of
his mouth : I could imagine him dragging these little dykes open
when shaving. He was dressed so conventionally that he might be
a judge, a diplomat, a shopwalker, a shipowner or an old-time
Shakespearian actor : black coat, striped trousers, grey spats, white

slip inside his waistcoat, butterfly collar folded deeply and a black cravat held by a gold clasp with a tiny diamond.

The backs of his fingers were hairy : he wore an amethyst ring almost as big as a bishop's. His temples were greying and brushed up in two sweeping wings – wherefore the suggestion of an actor. On the rack over his head was a leather hat-case with the initials 'F.J.N.' in Gothic lettering. He was obviously an Englishman who had crossed the night before. ("Up the Bare Stairs", *The Man Who Invented Sin*, p. 141).

These passages have been taken from stories written over a period of some twenty years. It cannot be asserted that they demonstrate all the ways in which O'Faolain portrays character. However, careful examination of them can lead to an awareness of differences in descriptive technique, of the writer's consistent, increasing endeavour to let the words he chooses do the work on their own, with less and less reliance on vocabulary which earlier was described as "Romantic allusive", and "Romantic visual".

The stories remain the property of the writer for as long as he is writing, but there may be a temptation – whether conscious or unconscious – to try to hold on to a story afterwards by wishing to make the reader see what is in the writer's mind by building in persuaders of one kind or another. The reader may therefore come to the story only at third or fourth remove. The writer has it first. He may then pass it on to a narrator who also often expresses an opinion, thereby possibly influencing the reader.

This may be noted in the first passage, where little clear information is given. O'Faolain is not setting a scene to be appreciated visually; the result is an emotional effect. Most of the descriptive words do not describe : they imply. The narrator sees the gypsy girl in terms of himself, so that while there are adjectives which establish her physical appearance, (e.g. "full"), such words do even more. Taken together with the other adjectives, the general, cumulative effect is not visual. The reader is led – wittingly or unwittingly – not so much to see the girl but to accept what the narrator feels about her. Although the narrator is not to be deliberately affected by or involved with the girl, even the surroundings and language are loaded with emotional association : the season (May), the dark night, the lighting which is provided by beams coming through a window. It is a "Gothic" window. The chestnuts do not scatter raindrops, but "benediction". This could be a scene from a sentimental novel : the fallen, abandoned woman, framed in the light from a window, shut out from society. The Gothic window might even suggest that she is standing outside a church. The associations which radiate from such

language are almost unlimited, even if they will tend to go in direc-
tions consciously or unconsciously predetermined by the author.

It will be helpful to refer to another passage in which again a
powerfully emotional effect is achieved :

> Looking at her soft eyes, and at her soft hair, my eyes wandered
> down to the first shadows of her breasts : she caught my glance
> and looked down at her warm bosom and then at me and she
> smiled. As I moved to her I saw the little broken corner of her
> tooth : I had no word to say; so I sat beside her before the leaping
> flames and put my arms around her and felt in the cup of my
> hollow palm the firm casque of her breast. Smiling at me as a sick
> woman might smile upon a doctor who brought her ease from
> pain she slipped my hand beneath her blouse to where I felt her
> warm protruding nipple, and I leaned to her for a kiss. ("Fugue",
> *FS*, p. 48).

The narrator (the author's medium) is telling what lies in front of
his eyes, so that the reader is able to form his own impression. Of
course the writer wishes to make the reader's mind work in a particular way, but in this case the scene has been set long in advance.
The boy and girl have met. The reader knows that they are attracted
to each other. There is no mystery, the relationship of the two young
people has been adequately (though not exhaustively) established.
Little is known or revealed about the gypsy girl, except that she is
Stevey Long's girl-friend and that she is worried.

There are still vague, suggestive words throughout the passage
from "Fugue" ("soft hair", "soft eyes"; in particular, "warm bosom").
The words help to convey not so much the physical attraction, but
the need of comfort on the part of the boy. "Bosom" suggests the
maternal, especially since a different term is used just before this, "the
first shadows of her breasts". There is an effective mixture of the
visual with the suggestive, which is not to imply that the visual may
not be suggestive too.

A little before this, the setting of the table and the preparations
for a simple meal have been mentioned. All of these carry with them
to the narrator and to the reader a feeling of being at home, out of
the cold, no longer on the run. Factual information is given, including
the comment that the girl's teeth are not regular, the implication
being that the girl is not just dreamed of, but visualised; she is
mortal, not sublime. The writer and reader do not take off for loftier,
dizzier heights where the mind no longer functions.

It is interesting now to switch to another passage in which the girl
makes her first entrance :

Used to this sort of thing, and pitying us, she came down, barefooted, her black hair around her, a black cloak on her shoulders not altogether drawn over her pale breast, a candle blown madly by the wind slanting in her hand. ("Fugue", *FS*, p. 37).

This time the light does not come from a source which in itself is suggestive. The girl carries a candle whose weak flame enables the narrator to see the girl in black, and not quite white. Her breast, for example, is described as "pale". This is a very good word here. "White" would have brought in associations (virginity, purity) which could lead to predetermination of the picture the reader creates for himself from the few details he is given. All the words are chosen to enable the reader to use the narrator's eyes without – because this is quite unnecessary – being distracted by what is in the narrator's mind. The only expression which might in the context seem a little intemperate is "madly". A small flame caught by even a breeze flickers wildly, so that "madly" is appropriate, accurate, and as a contrast to what precedes it, very effective. Altogether this paragraph faithfully records what is registered by somebody coming in from the dark. In the case of the gypsy, the approach is not direct. O'Faolain's use of the adjective "rich", when applied to the girl's hips, retrospectively considered, is ironic. At this point in the story its impact is different.

The extracts so far examined came from stories which have a narrator. Although there is no direct narrator in "Admiring the Scenery" the author stands very close behind the reader, never once letting the story get away on its own, constantly, though not always openly, influencing the way it is to be understood. In the passage quoted, for example, there are only three clear statements about Hanafan's appearance. His complexion is dark from shaving, he has wrinkles round his eyes, his lips are thin. All the rest is deduction on the part of the writer from these few facts. After this opening section, any mention of Hanafan or of what he does or says, is accompanied by words like "melancholy" or "gentle". The cumulative effect is for the reader to become more and more aware of a tragic happening in Hanafan's life. The writer is not content to let the facts speak for themselves because he is not prepared to reveal them all (particularly the one piece of information which would explain why Hanafan is a broken man) with the result that the writer has to bend everything in the story to establish a sense of total despair. O'Faolain sees not the event as such, but the effect on Hanafan, as being important. Hence nature, the weather, the language, the other characters, the literary allusions, the setting, the story within the story, all are mobilised to concentrate the reader's attention to the last on a figure broken by sorrow.

Close examination has shown that "Admiring the Scenery" is a very carefully constructed story. It is perhaps an example of that formality which may only be found in art, because art often demands a pattern which is never found in life.

It is almost with a sense of relief that one turns now to the passage from "Lady Lucifer" in which the doctor is introduced. This is the man who will later tell the story within the story. Not everything is related, but nowhere in this story can one find the almost subliminal technique noted in "Admiring the Scenery". Nor is the narrator the main character.

There are no words in the passage which carry emotional overtones. All that is said of the doctor is that he has sandy hair and that he has a good figure. His facial expression is referred to briefly, but not in the same manner as with Hanafan. The description of Hanafan is highly metaphorical, deliberately evasive. One is told that he is a teacher. That is all. In the case of the doctor, just a few details of his professional career are given. Nothing is said about the kind of man he is, except that he "bore himself with the authority of experience and power". This is not suggestion, but direct statement.

The doctor's features are only indirectly mentioned : "serious, but not severe". Description of physical appearance is kept to a minimum. This is very typical of twentieth century short stories, although not always of O'Faolain (as the passage from "Up the Bare Stairs" demonstrates). It is of course O'Faolain who writes these words, and even bald statements of fact suggest something. Here they do no more than conjure up the appearance and background of a man about whom there are no unanswered questions because none are posed or provoked.

Both in "Lady Lucifer" and "Up the Bare Stairs" a much more factually descriptive technique is employed, even though there is a narrator in "Up the Bare Stairs". He introduces Nugent ("my travelling companion"), looking at him across a railway compartment, attempting to imagine from what he sees, the kind of man Nugent is. Twice he makes statements in which he says what Nugent's appearance suggests : "He was dressed so conventionally that he might . . ." and "His temples were greying and brushed up in two sweeping wings – wherefore the suggestion of . . .". Neither of his assumptions is correct. There is no reason why they should be. He is only doing what any curious person might do when sharing a carriage with a stranger – he looks at that person, trying to deduce background and character from externalities. How different this is

from "Midsummer Night Madness" where the narrator on occasion
knows more than he should. For example, as has been seen already,
the narrator has no reason for referring to the girl's hips as "too
rich, too wide", unless – and that is not likely – he is judging the
girl's appearance from an aesthetic point of view. The remark could
then be interpreted as negative comment on the girl's figure. The
narrator, and through him the author, is indulging in language which
is initially confusing, only retrospectively to be understood as ironic.

In the description of Nugent, a statement is made – a very unequivocal one – which also turns out to be ironic : "He was obviously
an Englishman who had crossed the night before". Nugent is Irish.
Here the narrator seems to be basing his assumption on what he has
in front of him. It is perfectly reasonable for him to do so. Yet the
reader is being misled because the narrator knows that Nugent is not
English. In this instance the writer quite obviously wishes the reader
to feel his own way into the story. Nevertheless O'Faolain is playing
a kind of trick since he does not have to introduce Nugent in this
way. He could just as easily have told the reader who Nugent was
right from the start, so that even here, it is only an apparent lack of
interference on the part of the writer. Admittedly the mistaken
nationality is cleared up very early on in the story. It serves merely
to bring the reader to experience with the narrator, not to influence
the way the reader's mind will work.

This may be appreciated better if reference is once more made
to the technique of evasiveness examined earlier in "Admiring the
Scenery". Two examples will suffice. Hanafan is introduced with
the words, "There was nothing remarkable about this third man.".
There most certainly is. Even more striking is a statement which
comes later. Hanafan is talking about the station-master :

> . . . "he had no sense and the people used to make a hare of him.
> He couldn't sing any more than I could. He had a small little
> voice, a small range too, but it had no strength or sweetness;
> there was no richness in it."
> The teacher said these words, strength, sweetness, richness, with
> a luscious curl of his thin lips around the fruit of sound. His eyes
> widened. Clearly he was seeing nothing but the old station master.
> Earnestly he went on, a small glow on each cheek. ("Admiring
> the Scenery", FS, p. 107).

Perhaps Hanafan was seeing the station-master; the reader is
certainly being encouraged to think so. Yet the adverb "clearly"
must here be understood as a distractor, particularly as the language
used by Hanafan becomes increasingly emotional as he talks about

this one night. Since Hanafan was not related to the station-master, there is no reason at all for his excitement. The deliberately distractive intent behind the use of "clearly" is confirmed in the following sentence : "Earnestly he went on, a small glow on each cheek." Why should Hanafan be so roused by the memory of a foolish old man? The explanation must be that he is thinking of something else which he does not mention and which O'Faolain wishes to be withheld.

To return now to the description of Nugent, elsewhere in the introductory passage, there is – apart from the points already discussed – no evidence of the writer attempting to influence the reader. Physical details are given, also details of dress from which the narrator proceeds to draw conclusions as to the man's profession and background. O'Faolain stresses the unremarkability – although he does not say Nugent was unremarkable : "He was dressed so conventionally that he might be . . ." There is a marked lack of metaphorical expression. The adjectives employed are simple, ("bull-shouldered", "coarse", "sallow", "deep", "little", "black", "striped", "grey", "white") they do not have anything more than their usual meaning. In contrast to the doctor ("Lady Lucifer") Nugent's features are dwelt on at some length. In both cases the effect is visual, the reader being offered a greater or lesser amount of information on which to build up his own impression. Here he is neither overtly nor unconsciously being influenced by the writer – except and in so far as everything in the story comes from O'Faolain.

The doctor's two friends are introduced equally briefly;

In the stern the priest lay like Velasquez's picture of "Old Silenus lolling in the sunshine", his bare paunch, immensely pink, spilling over his black trousers . . .

The clerk was only a bank clerk by avocation : his inward life was in his writing; he wrote novels and stories, over the name of Malachy Lucas. ("Lady Lucifer", pp. 121–123).

If one again thinks back to the introduction of the other two men in "Admiring the Scenery", one is immediately struck by the differences. Here all that one learns of the priest is that he is fat, an impression which is emphasized through the comparison with Silenus. O'Faolain makes a point of explaining that the comparison comes not from him, but from the clerk ("It was he who had said that the priest was like old Silenus") almost suggesting that the writer no longer wishes to use such imagery, or does not intend that the reader shall be unconsciously influenced. Of course there is a further possibility that O'Faolain's ascribing the remark to the clerk could be interpreted as reflecting more on Malachy than on the priest. Malachy is a dreamy, introspective man to whom such remarks come naturally. Elsewhere, both in the early and later work, O'Faolain also compares his characters with models chosen from the arts – the Scottish girl ("The Silence of the Valley") with Beethoven, Barbara ("A Sweet Colleen") with Rossetti.

Of the priest in "Admiring the Scenery" O'Faolain says that he was a man who had, "finally solved his problems in a spirit of good-humoured regret." In this story it was noticed that certain adjectives ("sad" and "gentle") accompanied both Hanafan and the priest through the story, so that these attributes came to be associated with the two men. This does not happen in "Lady Lucifer", although it would be untrue to assert that O'Faolain no longer employs such devices in other stories. In her chapter on "Unholy Living and Half Dying", Suzanne Dockrell-Grünberg has shown how O'Faolain, while writing in a seemingly light-hearted manner, can all the time keep referring to a central point in the story – death. The relationship of the apparently dying landlady and the apparently robust lodger is presented in simple everyday terms, and yet, as Suzanne Dockrell-Grünberg explains :

> Das eindrucksvolle Erlebnis der Karfreitagnacht läßt selbst bei Tage noch eine Spur von Furcht zurück. Die Worte seines Freundes : ". . . the stamp is on you . . ." klingen in ihm als Warnung nach. Die Bemerkung zeigt in ihrer Doppeldeutigkeit (konkret das Klopfen, im übertragenen Sinn die Kirche) die beiden durchgehenden Strömungen in dieser Short Story : die Darstellung des Geschehens selbst und die dadurch ausgelöste Steigerung der Angst, die sich aus der plötzlichen Konfrontierung mit dem Tod ergibt. Angst in der alten Frau in dem Augenblick, als sie glaubt, sterben zu müssen; Angst in Cardew durch die umgehende Atmosphäre und die Erkenntnis seiner inneren Leere. Angst in seinen Freunden, die sich an ihre Pflichten gemahnt fühlen. Jedder sucht die Ungewissheit, die gemeinsame Angst auf seine Art zu betäuben : seine Freunde durch ihre eilige Beichte; die Alte durch übertriebene Frömmigkeit; Cardew durch seinen wachsenden Widerstand gegenüber der Kirche und Ihren Institutionen. (*Studien zur Struktur Moderner Anglo-Irischer Short Stories*, p. 132).

In this story it is not so much the repetition of the same adjectives which helps the writer to establish the mood in the mind of the reader, but rather by using words or allusions which have to do with death, or which could be seen as having to do with death, that O'Faolain successfully builds up a sense of the mortality of all things.

The objects and people around Cardew are mute yet expressive witnesses to the fact that he and they must pass away ("the stamp is on you", "the dying fire", "hollowed cheeks", "slow as a hearse", "faint knocking", "intense vacancy", "low tide"). While making such a statement, one must also realise that there is a difference between constantly referring to a character in a story as "gentle" or "sad", and surrounding him with objects and people, or having things happen to him, which remind him that he too will die. In both cases the reader may come to an awareness of the truth which the writer is offering through his story. Nevertheless, the reader does have a choice in "Unholy Living and Half Dying". Although O'Faolain is responsible for every word in the story, he still leaves it to the reader to interpret the signs, to take the hints – if he wishes to.

Even the beginning of the story, where Jacky Cardew is introduced, is not as unequivocal as it might at first appear :

> Jacky Cardew is one of those club bachelors who are so well-groomed, well-preserved, pomaded, medicated, and self-cosseted that they seem ageless – the sort of fixture about whom his pals will say when he comes unstuck around the age of eighty, "Well, well! didn't poor old Jacky Cardew go off very fast at the end?" ("Unholy Living and Half Dying", *FS*, p. 201).

This is a humorous, colloquial description. Physical details are given, but they suggest a type rather than an individual. Again it is up to the reader to imagine for himself. Nugent, although O'Faolain devotes nearly a page to his description, is not more present than Cardew. Both men are given exteriors which would comfortably fit many of a certain type.

In "Lady Lucifer" and "Up the Bare Stairs", the story is taken up by one of the main figures, although not immediately. This is particularly interesting in the case of "Up the Bare Stairs". The narrator ("I") says not a word until Nugent has finished telling the story of his life, another example of the writer permitting the story to take its own course, of not endeavouring to over-ensure that the reader's thoughts will move in the right direction. In "A Broken World", a much earlier story, the narrator constantly interrupts, talks and argues with the other characters, has an opinion which he expresses. He also sums up at the end. Nugent has his say without interruption. Afterwards the two men talk to each other for a few minutes before the train comes into the station. The narrator makes no final comments on what he has heard. The story closes with the narrator looking on as Nugent leaves the train and meets his relations on the platform.

The doctor ("Lady Lucifer") tells the story of the asylum to illustrate a remark which he makes: "Pride and humility aren't opposites. They're two sides of the same thing." There is no reason for supposing that the doctor was personally involved in what happened at the asylum – or only in his professional capacity as a doctor. He obviously finds the woman in the tragedy attractive, but afterwards, in what he says when telling the story, it seems that he stands outside the affair which he uses merely in support of his argument. He tells the whole story, so far as one can judge. Hanafan, for example, left out one essential – what happened on that one night in the past. However there is a rather curious tendency on the part of the doctor and Nugent to describe others in language which is reminiscent of the early stories. For example, the doctor talking of the girl at the asylum:

> She was a beautiful girl. Tall as a spear. Dark as night. Her two eyes were two brown jewels set under her forehead. She was one of the most beautiful girls I have ever seen. (LL, p. 129).

This is imagery which in theory should make the reader's mind work, since it is highly allusive. Expressions such as "Tall as a spear. Dark as night" are suggestive but they do not in fact lead the reader to try to imagine what the girl really looked like. Should he do so, he would become bewildered. "Spears", "night", "jewels", an accumulation of images, all trying very hard to convey beauty, instead, through the quick sequence of different nouns, tending to confuse rather than enlighten or clarify. These words could suggest all kinds of ideas: the mysterious, the East, almost the supernatural. Indeed when the doctor first refers to the girl he says "She was like a goddess dressed in a wave."

In talking of Davidson, the doctor uses similar, if somewhat modified language: "Davidson, a gentle drooping fellow with a girlish complexion." This inferential description is repeated later: "I remember Davidson asking him about Africa, in his soft, drooly voice."

Additional points emerge from the references to Davidson. He loves the girl but is not loved by her. He cannot break with her, nor, when he is the only one to notice that Motherway (who returns to the asylum after a period of years and is about to marry the girl) is mad, does he say anything. He is "soft" in that he cannot tell the girl the truth. Retrospectively there is even a sinister, tragic, ring to the repetitive description of Davidson in such terms. Here one might see chinks in the hard, or apparently hard, shell of the doctor. He has made his way in life. So has Nugent. But at what cost? They are both capable of deep feeling, have learned to be mistrustful of it. Perhaps that is the reason why both, when describing others in a crisis situation, indulge in language which is emotional. For example, when Nugent mentions Angelo – even the names, Angelo, Mother-way, have clear associations –

> There was a time when I thought he was the nicest little man in the whole school. Very handsome. Cheeks as red as a girl, black bristly hair, blue eyes and the most perfect teeth I've ever seen between a man's lips. (UTBS, p. 144).

The suggestion appears to be that feminine features on a man are dangerous. Davidson is also described as "girlish". Both Davidson and Angelo are innocents who are easily injured. Perhaps theirs is the kind of innocence which Graham Greene so often attacks. For Greene, the fact of not knowing, or of being unaware, is considered inexcusable, punishable. In *The Quiet American*, Pyle's ingenuous attitude to Communism results in the killing of women and children. Neither Davidson nor Angelo is guilty of sins of this magnitude. Both however fail to act at moments of crisis, so that those towards whom they are emotionally attracted are hurt.

Elsewhere too, this negative innocence may be read into physical appearance. In "The Man Who Invented Sin", for example:

> Brother Majellan was very different, a gentle, apple-cheeked man with big glasses, a complexion like a girl, teeth as white as a hound's, and soft, beaming eyes. He was an intelligent, beaming man. (*The Man Who Invented Sin*, p. 4).

Even Hanafan is briefly referred to in this way: "his oblong face . . . delicate as a woman's." Later in the story Majellan is censured by the narrator for refusing to see that in spite of what the local priest had pretended, there was no guilt attached to the relationship of the two nuns and two monks during those happy weeks spent together many years before.

However there is a difference. "The Man Who Invented Sin" is told by a narrator throughout. In "Up the Bare Stairs" and "Lady Lucifer", Angelo, Davidson, Motherway and the girl are described by Nugent and the doctor, who enter the story after the beginning. Whereas both men generally speak modestly, eschewing the flamboyant, the moment they start to relate the past, their language changes. There are at least two sides to their personalities. The softer side, the side they do not often show, is still there. In this instance its existence is revealed through the passion expressed in their diction. It may be remembered that Hanafan's appearance and language also change when he talks about the past. The contrast here is between a man who is aware of the emotions, who gives them their due – if limited – place and a Hanafan who is broken by his sensitive nature.

Delineation of character in depth is not attempted in "Up the Bare Stairs" and "Lady Lucifer". The incidents, other characters, background, conversations, all are so chosen to have a bearing on the central statement. Hence the two other men in "Lady Lucifer" are shown in contrast to the doctor. They have not taken up the challenge of life. From what he says, it seems that the priest has taken refuge in the church. If he could, the clerk would act similarly by settling in the country where he feels he would have the right surroundings for inspiration.

The doctor is clearly aware of the state of mind of his two friends. When the three of them discuss where they would ideally like to live and the two others express a desire to retire to the country, the doctor interjects :

"Lucas, you're not much over thirty. Isn't it a bit early to want to renounce the world?" The priest grinned. "I renounced the world at twenty-four." (LL, p. 123).

The verb "renounce" is repeated twice in this paragraph – a word which implies a deliberate decision to opt out of life. Furthermore the implications of standing still, of not wishing to face reality, go even further. The two men may be considered against the larger background of Ireland and the Irish. O'Faolain quotes the example of Liam O'Flaherty (through the doctor) – a man who left Ireland – and of the stories he wrote of those who remained behind :

"The daft ones stayed at home and went into the woods and wrote poetry. Take care, Lucas." (LL, p. 124).

The good physique of the doctor is mentioned several times ("finely-built", "soldierly") whereas the priest is very fat. May there not in this be more than a suggestion that not entering the world, brings with it both mental and physical decay? In this story, the other characters – particularly the two friends – are foils to the doctor. Whereas Hanafan and the priest in "Admiring the Scenery" were linked by common adjectives, here it is the differences which the reader is able to appreciate for himself.

It is perhaps even possible to see here that central split in character which Conrad reveals in his major novels; that danger-point which lies between the life of the imagination and the life which is kept firmly under control, where the calls of duty and common sense keep the door bolted and barred on doubts and hesitation.

NATURE : SETTING

As in many of the early stories, nature forms the background for "Lady Lucifer" : three men go out into the country. Once again it is possible to discern differences in technique if comparisons are made with the first stories. In "Midsummer Night Madness" nature was seen to be almost a character in its own right, the narrator on occasion even identifying himself with nature. The overwhelming presence of early summer, combined with the youthfulness of the narrator, result in a continuing, increasing sense of the almost physical relationship between man and nature. The writer was felt to be urging the reader to participate directly in the sensual atmosphere established by the narrator with all that surrounds him. In stories which follow, particularly in "Admiring the Scenery", nature is still constantly in evidence, although it is no longer personified, or not to such a degree.

In "Admiring the Scenery" nature was defined as a "mood reflector", in that adjectives used to describe Hanafan are also applied to the countryside. The writer is clearly (though not obviously) influencing what the reader will think. Not only the outward appearance of nature is conjured up, but also the mood which this appearance suggests to the writer. Even things past are recaptured through the face of nature. For example, Hanafan retains an almost photographic memory of the winter night of long before. When he is once more in the same place his mind switches back effortlessly, the scene is recovered intact .The joy felt on that occasion is dead, although it is re-kindled just for the period of Hanafan's narration. O'Faolain consciously links nature with the mood of loneliness and sadness which pervades this whole story. Descriptive words are used which go beyond the simple visual. This may be seen more clearly if passages from "Midsummer Night Madness" and "Admiring the Scenery" are placed beside sections from "Lady Lucifer":

> Then, mounting my bicycle, I turned to the open fields and drew in a long draught of their sweetness, their May-month sweetness, as only a man could who had been cooped up for months past under one of those tiny roofs . . . and rode on happily into

the country . . . Fallen hawthorn blossoms splashed with their
lime the dust of the road, and so narrow were the boreens in
places that the lilac and the dog rose, hung with wisps of hay,
reached down as if to be plucked. Under the overhanging trees
I could smell the pungent smell of the laurel sweating in the damp
night air. And all about me the dead silence of the coming night,
the heavy silence, drowsy with the odors of the night flowers and
the cut meadows, unless a little stream trickled over the road and
my wheels made a great double splash as they crossed it. ("Midsummer Night Madness", *FS*, pp. 1–2).

The priest nodded. The small man looked contemptuously at
Hanafan, who now began to quote from Gray's "Elegy" in his
round womanly voice, all the time looking sadly at the warmth of
the sun fading from the distant grains of snow, and the mountain
becoming black and cold. ("Admiring the Scenery", *FS*, p. 105).

The three friends had rowed very slowly down-river – half-
floated, indeed – seeing only the withered thistles in the fields,
cows standing to their ankles in still water. There was not a speck
in the sky. Not even a bird; as if they had taken shelter from the
humming heat in the pine-forest that rose on one side, dark and
cool as a cave. The only sound they heard for a mile was the fall
of water in the canal-lock; and when they passed through the
lock and were lazily poling along the slim perspective of the canal,
everything was again sloth and softness and sun. The narrow
road of canal was a dreaming slip of water. They were secluded,
lost, tucked away. The world had died . . .

As they rocked gently along, these two jungles of river-plants
undulated faintly – balsam, golden flags, willow-herb, coltsfoot,
purple loose-strife : their delicate pungency scented the warm air.
Nobody spoke . . .

In front they saw a toy lock-house perched beside a tiny hump-
backed bridge; that, and the much-tarred warehouse nearby meant
that another shallows lay ahead . . . ("Lady Lucifer", pp. 121–122).

There can be no doubt that in all of these passages nature reflects
a mood. It is possible however to discern a continuing movement
away from the direct personal to a more controlled, mediate method
of presentation.

Whereas in "Midsummer Night Madness", nature is experienced
almost physically, in "Admiring the Scenery" changes in time with
Hanafan's alternating moods – these changes being intimated by the
writer, not by Hanafan, in language which still has echoes of earlier
work – in "Lady Lucifer", careful examination seems to show that
the writer is at pains to create the impression that the setting of the

story reveals itself to the eyes of the reader and is not pre-determined by the writer.

How does O'Faolain achieve a seeming absence? Above all he writes through the three men ("The three men had rowed . . ."). He records, very accurately, what they experience, emphasizing that it is they who register what is around them, by constantly repeating this ("they heard", "they were secluded", "they rocked", "they saw").

Although the general effect of the passage is to establish an almost tangible sense of the surroundings and of suspended animation, the words and images chosen to accomplish this are almost exclusively negative ("Not a speck", "not even a bird", "The only sound", "They . . . were lost", "the world had died", "withered thistles", "everything was sloth"). What a contrast this is to the passage from "Midsummer Night Madness" where the sentences almost explode with the exuberance of associations touched off by the power of nature.

There is a double purpose behind the passage from "Lady Lucifer". The outer appearance, the long stretch of water shimmering in the heat is clearly, visually presented. Negatives stop the text from rising above the desired emotional level. The writer is in no danger of letting his feelings run away with the reader.

There are some isolated expressions which carry more positive associations with them ("softness", "dreaming slip"). The word "softness" seems perhaps a little inappropriate. It is not a very precise noun. Here, in a description of a day when the sun is beating down, one is tempted to assume that it was chosen rather for its sound ("sloth", "softness", "sun") than for its accuracy. The other expression, "The narrow road of the canal was a dreaming slip of water", can stand by itself. Although the canal is personified, in context it tends to establish nature as an entity on its own, with no reference to the three men passing over its surface, or to the writer. Admittedly two of the men are dreamers. Is not this once more a statement which may be seen at two completely separate levels? It is to be taken at face value as something which is felt by the beholder. It may later come to be understood as part of that Irish background, that lotus life so ridiculed by the doctor.

In this introductory section, the reader is enabled, by being approached through the three men, to come into the story without necessarily thinking of the three men or being directly influenced by the writer. The progress the men make, the objects they pass, the almost imperceptible motion, all these are enumerated, explained in several ways. For example the leisurely speed at which they proceed is variously indicated : the lengthy sentences, words which suggest immobility or lethargy, the long vowels and onomatopœic phrases ("the only sound they heard for a mile was the fall of water . . . lazily poling along the slim perspective . . . sloth, and softness and sun . . ."). Certain words and phrases are repeated ("lost", "slowly", "dud-dudding") indicative of the regular sounds which accompany life in the country; also its sameness.

In this story O'Faolain is demonstrably following his own dictum :

Realistic detail, in short, is a bore if it merely gives us an idle verisimilitude : its function is to be a part of this general revelation by suggestion. (*The Short Story*, p. 163).

There is no doubt that O'Faolain does offer realistic detail in this first paragraph of the story. Although the scene is one of idleness, it is certainly not idle verisimilitude since, if the senses are not intoxicated, neither are they confused with over-fanciful imagery. In fact, it is more an atmosphere than a mood which is established at the beginning, an atmosphere which is purely physical, implying at this stage of the story no more than the fact that the day is hot, that as a result, those exposed to it are lethargic.

O'Faolain manages in the course of the story to link the slowness of life, the indifference to progress, with certain Irish attitudes expressed by the doctor and the other two men : the argument, as has been seen in earlier stories, of whether to go forward or backward; the country representing the backward look, the city, where modern man has to find his place. The countryside, in an age which has long since abandoned any meaningful contact with nature, is depicted as the repository for dreams, a retreat for the unthinking and unambitious.

One might even make the paradoxical claim that O'Faolain regards nature as a source of negative inspiration. What he does not do – except in one revealing passage at the end – is express his (the writer's) feelings directly through nature. While the descriptive passages may carry many meanings, they do not harbour hidden persuaders.

Generally speaking things are seen for what they are, are presented directly. The reader is left to infer for himself. Where comment is made, it comes from one of the characters. The doctor is not afraid to state his mind, and does so in no uncertain terms. For example, each time one of the other two men talks about returning to the country for ever, the doctor attacks immediately. When Lucas admires the lock-house, the doctor tells him how dark and smoky it is. He notices that the young woman who lives at the lock-house has teeth which need attention. It is he who probes, to discover how un-

H

comfortable the house is in winter, with water on the ground-floor and a boat moored in the garden. His questions are all answered in an unintelligent or completely uninterested manner. When asked whether she would prefer to live in the town the woman merely replies, "I dunno, sir." At the end when the doctor points out to the woman that the paper she has just brought in is a day old, she answers "Ah, . . . sure it's all wan to us."

There is however a possibility of reading a little more into one or two of the descriptions of the house. It is first referred to as a "toy" lock-house, with a "tiny hump-backed", (later "humpty-dumpty") bridge. The three friends have been drifting down the river enveloped in a shimmering heat haze. Out of this, the small house suddenly emerges. Again, the metaphor can be interpreted visually, although considered in the light of what is said of country life, there could be other, negative radiations as well. In "A Broken World" it will be remembered how the priest constantly mentions the harmony of a world which no longer exists. He refers to his experience of looking across a broad valley, seeing how everything, the houses, the landscape, merge and blend. There is no such unity in "Lady Lucifer". The inside of the house too is brought to the reader as if he were entering it with the three men :

> The plain, low-ceilinged kitchen was so dim that the usual red lamp before the usual oleograph of the Sacred Heart was a brilliant eye of scarlet. It was cool after the great heat outside. A gun and a fishing-rod hung over the mantlepiece; thighboots broken-necked in a corner; a scythe behind the door; over a pannier of plums wasps rose and sank and folded their wings to glut. The young woman was friendly, but shy. (LL, p. 125).

Once in the cool, dark interior, they look out :

> Through the tiny window they saw the barge nose into the lock. One of the crew leaned his back against the beam of the gate and slowly slewed it against the flood. Another, at the other end, worked the winch. It took a long time. Slowly the stovepipe began to sink below the level of the lock-wall. (LL, p. 126).

There is clear evidence of the effectiveness of repetition, of using words to suggest the languid measured unhurried pace of life, the fastidiousness of detail, the sense of retarded movement ("nose", "slowly", "leaned", "slowly", "slewed", "long time", "slowly", "sink"). These are all words with unambiguous meanings. How do the priest and Malachy react to this?

"How nice to think," mused the clerk, elbows on the table as he sipped his tea, "that they've been doing that for a hundred and fifty years. No wonder life gets into a little rut." "Aye, to be sure!" the priest agreed contentedly, lighting his pipe. "Everything here is old. Old and traditional. That turf-fire. The fishing-rod. The scythe. They don't need much to live. A bit of turf, a couple of fish, a wild duck, a bite of hay for the cow. It's an attractive sort of existence, Doc. And isn't it better anyway than a slum in Dublin?' (LL, p. 126).

"I'm not saying that everybody should leave the country and go into the city. That would be absurd. What I'm talking about is people deliberately trying to bury themselves away somewhere. Lucas imagines he'd like it. You really wouldn't, you know. Anybody with ambitions has to live a full life. Anybody with a bit of pride in him. You'd run out of it in a month." (LL, p. 127).

Taken together, these passages show that what the writer has in mind is not the depiction of an idyll, but the bursting of a bubble. Once again the central idea and all the parts of the puzzle are either introduced through one of the characters, or may be seen to fit into a larger scheme of things. The doctor, acting mediately, is already starting to work towards the heart of the story when he mentions the word "pride". He later goes on to say that pride and humility are but two sides of the same coin. Pride and humility are perceptible in the contrasts : between the doctor and the two other men, between the town and the country, between looking to the past and looking to the future, between ambition and lack of it, and between those involved in the tragedy at the asylum.

In the three passages quoted, O'Faolain goes into the house with the three men, although not so that his presence is felt. They register what is there. They look out of the window, to become aware of how life slowly passes the house (and them) by. The clerk talks of a "rut". The priest "contentedly" agrees with him. The doctor goes on to remind them once again of the foolishness of burying oneself alive.

In the light of the reactions of the three men to the house, what is the reader likely to conclude? He is not obliged to, but if he reflects on the interior of the house, and particularly on the way the clerk and the priest talk about it, he may well begin to wonder if the setting is not deliberate cliché. All the objects mentioned : the sacred heart, the scythe, the turf-fire, the fishing rod, the gun, are what one would expect to find on a picture postcard depicting the typical Irish cottage.

Up to this moment, neither the clerk nor the priest has stopped, or dared, to question his aspirations. They have quietly, undramatically given up. Every word they utter reveals this. The author just lets setting, dialogue and actions speak for themselves. For example, even where O'Faolain refers to Malachy's occupation, he says :

> The clerk was only a bank-clerk by avocation : his inward life was in his writings. (LL, p. 122).

This explains a state of affairs, not a state of mind. There is no insistence. Some facts are given, the reader must do the rest for himself.

It will be remembered that in "Up the Bare Stairs" there is even a conscious, explicit refusal to let nature come into the story at all, when Nugent is described as showing just a "casual interest in the countryside" from the train, before indifferently shutting his eyes. He too, having left Ireland years before, being completely urbanised, the softer side burnt out of his system in youth, is not excited at the sight of the countryside. Only at the end does his attitude change; then only as the train approaches his native town.

> His eyes lit up. I looked sideways to see what had arrested him. It was the first lights of Cork, and, mingling with the smoke over the roofs, the January night. Behind the violet hills the last cinder of the sun made a saffron horizon. As the train roared into the tunnel we could see children playing in the streets below the steep embankment, and he was staring at them thirstily . . . (UTBS, p. 152).

Nugent is not to be distracted by appearances which are of no relevance to him. O'Faolain does not attempt wrongly to use the countryside to fill out the character of a man who has never had any contact with it.

This may help to explain why nature is made a part – a very important part – of "Lady Lucifer". All three men live lives which have nothing to do with the countryside, so that O'Faolain is more or less forced – if he is to achieve verisimilitude – to be very circumspect in introducing nature into such a story. Generally he is successful in avoiding the obvious pitfalls, of not permitting himself to be so carried away by the thought of nature as to make his figures behave out of character, or ease the strict control which references to and descriptions of nature here demand.

And yet there is still the final section of the story to be explained, including the doctor's last words as the three men go slowly homewards : "Dear God," he gasped, "This is heaven ! Heaven !" This may seem a strange remark from a man who has all along been preaching a message of restraint, of non-involvement in the beauties of nature. It is explicable, without contradicting what has so far been argued. The doctor can look round at the countryside illumined by the setting sun, yet still see it with eyes which remain unblinded. His is the response of a man who can take pleasure in his surroundings without being deluded into interpreting falsely what he sees. He is aware that nature can offer him relaxation, aesthetic delight, but that it is not the place in which he can realise any kind of professional ambitions.

How different is the attitude of the priest and the clerk :

The priest lay in the stern, his heavy chin on his chest, his eyes fixed heavily on the clerk. "Life is a divil," breathed the clerk. (LL, p. 140).

For them nature stimulates sentimental notions of what they have missed in life. They remain dreamers, unsatisfied, frustrated, unfulfilled.

In this story nature still has a place. It is not just a convenient background, a pretty setting. An atmosphere is created from the beginning, a sentimental bubble blown, exploded. Yet even while working through the visual, O'Faolain is often able to leave other options open. For example :

In the distance of the canal they saw the barge drawing its arrowy wake after it, and all along the way as it receded the river-plants on either side bowed their heads deep into the water and slowly swung upwards again when the arrows had passed on. (LL, p. 140).

This passage may be considered in a purely visual sense. The reader will have no difficulty in imagining the scene for himself. There are other meanings which may legitimately be drawn from what is said – or rather, from what is not said. May one not find here a further, oblique reference to the lethargy engendered by nature, or taken further still, by the "traditional" Irish way of life? It is reminiscent – though differently presented – of a scene towards the end of "A Broken World" in which the narrator watches the priest leaving the train, being greeted by his obsequious parishioners :

A manservant, touching his cap, took the bags. The stationmaster touched his cap to him. The porter receiving the tickets touched his cap to him. The jarvey, who was waiting for him, bowed as he received the bags from the manservant. Black, tall, thin, and straight as a lamp post, he left the lit, snow-bright station with every down-looking lounger there bowing and hat-touching as he passed. ("A Broken World", *FS*, p. 78).

In this last passage, the narrator emphasizes a statement made by the priest that the local people are much too "respectful". In the "Lady Lucifer" extract, it is left to the reader to decide what the writer intends. Even the repeated metaphor ("arrowy", "arrows") may be explained in terms of what the reader is expected to visualise. As the barge proceeds, the wake has the appearance of arrows, particularly at a distance. Reference back once more can show how even metaphorical language becomes more clearly definable, more easily understood at the visual level. In "Midsummer Night Madness", the narrator talks about driving the revolutionaries out "into the darkness, now rain-arrowy and old". This metaphorical formulation is not so easy to interpret. Such expressions tend to appeal primarily to the emotions, rather less to conjure up a distinct mental picture.

It is very tempting when following a particular line of thought to look only for evidence which will support this, to overlook, or choose to ignore anything which would contradict it. So far in this chapter it has been argued that in much of O'Faolain's later work, he departs from the emotional language to be found in many of the first stories. Yet even where the writer may be clearly seen to exercise the most rigorous control over what he writes, occasionally something of the earlier manner creeps in. O'Faolain himself would probably be the first to admit such discrepancies. He says in the Foreword to the *Finest Stories* :

> They (the last stories) started out to be satirical; they mostly failed dismally to be satirical; largely I presume – I observe it to my dismay and I confess it to my shame – because I still have much too soft a corner for the old land. For all I know I may still be a besotted romantic. (*FS*, pp. x-xi).

What happens in "Lady Lucifer"? The style is not completely consistent. There must be and is a difference in the language used by the writer to narrate, and that of the doctor. At the beginning a more mediate approach was noted. It might almost be said that the introduction succeeds not because of, but in spite of, what the text expresses.

Here too, a comparison may help to show differences. At the end of the passage quoted from "Midsummer Night Madness" come the following sentences :

Under the overhanging trees I could smell the pungent smell of the laurel sweating in the damp night air. And all about me the dead silence of the coming night, the heavy silence, drowsy with the odors of the night flowers and the cut meadows, unless a little stream . . . (*FS*, p. 2).

from "Lady Lucifer" :

As they rocked gently along, these two jungles of river-plants undulated faintly – balsam, golden flags, willow-herb, coltsfoot, purple loose-strife : their delicate pungency scented the warm air.

In the section from "Midsummer Night Madness" the narrator is recreating the effect on him (this is passed on to the reader directly) of being out on a night in May. The narrator sees, smells, and above all, feels. Hence what is observed is reproduced by feelings rather than by clear objects. The effects are achieved by means of repetitions, onomatopoeia, a mixture of the named ("laurel") with the intangible, imaginative, associative (e.g. "night flowers"), the vague but suggestive adjectives ("dead", "heavy", "heavy").

The narrator is writing about what he has experienced. He sees this only in terms of himself. Overtly – even if unconsciously – he coaxes the reader to accept his interpretation of what has happened to him.

How different the presentation – not necessarily the ultimate effect – is in the second extract. There are no words (even expressions like "jungle" or "scented") which are not easily understood. The flowers are given their proper names, not collected under a fanciful metaphor. The three men are not so much a part of the scene, but are shown passing through it. Even adverbs like "faintly" or "gently" suggest nothing more than the way the boat and the plants moved. ("Midsummer Night Madness" : "The summer night was falling as gently as dust").

In the first passage, it isn't enough that the laurel should be "pungent"; it must also "sweat in the damp night air", whereas : ". . . their delicate pungency scented the warm air" just continues the factual description which precedes it. Each of the words here carries a meaning which is clear, without any metaphorical or authorial associations. Once again it must be stressed that no attempt is being made to suggest that one method is better than another. Both of these passages are effective.

Another example of O'Faolain eschewing the deliberately metaphorical may be found at the beginning of the story : "The three friends rowed very slowly down-river – half-floated, indeed – ".

"Float" is a verb which will be found all through O'Faolain's writings. Elsewhere – and by no means only in the early stories – it is very often employed figuratively :

> The damp of dawn . . . floated over the rumbling river . . . ("Fugue", *FS*, p. 35).
> His dark vision passed out of his sight and he felt she had merely floated before him . . . ("The Patriot", *FS*, p. 52).
> . . . she soon found that the island floated on kindness. ("Lovers of the Lake", *FS*, p. 318).

In the example from "Lady Lucifer", the word "floated" merely indicates that the men were carried along with the current. The word is used in the normal dictionary sense. Although "half" is added to "floated" this just indicates that the current is so weak that the three men need only touch the oars to keep the boat moving. In a world which "had died" it would not have been surprising to find "float" introduced metaphorically. Against a background of quivering heat, suspended animation, the boat's progress might well have been described in a less exact manner.

The effect desired by the writer is successfully achieved in the opening section. Yet while this effect may be intentional, it will not be felt to be coming directly from him. Rather will the reader join the three men, become a part of the scene by creating it for himself.

It is very revealing to turn now to a short passage at the end :

> They entered the dim lane of the canal. It was now a long soft smudge – the flowers, the water, the woods. Only the ridge of the woods caught the sun. Their deeps were warmed by the moon. The evening birds were singing like mad. As the doctor poled he let out a deep sigh of joy. (LL, p. 140).

Nearly everything here is expressed in imagery which is the opposite of the visual. The canal is no longer just a canal, but "a dim lane, . . . a long soft smudge". Admittedly the day is ending, the light going. This is not what the writer evokes. The doctor is about to say, "This is heaven ! Heaven !" with which the story is concluded. O'Faolain is anticipating a little, directly urging the reader to feel the woods without seeing the trees. The imagery becomes increasingly extravagant : "Their deeps were warmed by the moon." Considered logically this is something of a mixed metaphor since the moon is cold. It is the moon which traditionally conveys or inspires romantic notions. The birds are "evening birds" ("Midsummer Night Madness", "night flowers").

In this passage it is possible to note an easing in the control which the author has elsewhere strictly exercised over descriptions of nature. This will be better appreciated if this passage is examined together with others in which the doctor mentions nature at times of crisis at the asylum. Here the same highly metaphorical diction occurs.

There is one other way in which nature is used in this story which has so far not been referred to : humour. Humour often implies an attempt – either conscious or unconscious – to be objective, or at least not to be overtly subjective. In an earlier chapter, nature was shown to be functioning as a mood reflector. In a story which has been seen to contain much that is mediate, humour may be seen as making its contribution to this.

> It is a lost corner, barely coming to life, some dim noise half-heard through sleep, a moth on a window-pane at morning, an occasional barge slowly dud-dudding along the river, disturbing the coots and the wild flowers with its arrowy wake. The very air of this deep valley seems too heavy to move. Even then a little cloud lay on the tip of the far line of mountains, too exhausted to persist. The doctor threw a plum-stone into the water. A heron rose from an island and flapped away in bored sloth into the woods. (LL, p. 123).

The cloud and the heron are personified in a mildly humorous way, as a reflection of the state of inanition which hangs over the entire countryside. Nature may be interpreted almost as a neutral commentator, certainly as not appearing to pass on the immediate feelings of the writer. This can be demonstrated even more strikingly from another story in the same collection, where the sound of waves is likened to an ironic chuckle. When Teresa and Patrick are walking beside the sea one afternoon and Teresa maliciously mentions gluttony as one of the sins committed by the nuns – an obvious reference to her companion's own weakness – the text continues :

> The little wavelets fell almost inaudibly, drunken with the fullness of the tide, exhausted and soothed by their own completion. (Teresa, FS, p. 197).

The angry silence is filled with the tiny sounds of the waves lapping against the shore. The reader is not expected to think of the sea visually. Quite obviously the intention is to provide a chorus, mute but expressive, which underlines the mood of the moment.

Later Stories II

LANGUAGE AND MEANING

Realistic detail, in short, is a bore if it merely gives us an idle verisimilitude : its function is to be part of this general revelation by suggestion. It is a fruitful realism when external reality releases the imagination : it is a barren realism when a reader says, "I could almost see that tree; or smell that pond." Why should anybody want *almost* to see a tree or smell a pond when he can go out in the fields and see a real tree and smell a real pond? Nowhere so much as in a short story are such irrelevant descriptions out-of-place; there is no time for them : however striking they may be they are among the many things which have to be dropped in this general struggle to make a very tiny part do for the whole. (Sean O'Faolain, *The Short Story*, p. 163).

I cannot help thinking that the factually meticulous realistic style is a step backwards technically (away from this engrosed alertness) though, in my taste, it is a brutal and spiritless and sluggish weapon at all times. Wherever there is wit, or an imaginative stir of humour or passion, or concentration of feeling or observation, we will find the more suggestive language leaping across deserts of literalness, and we chase after it to its glittering oasis. (Ibid, p. 233).

The two quotations at the head of this chapter illustrate one major problem for the short story writer in the twentieth century. The short story has been refined, has had such limits – above all of language – imposed on it, that for writers who have a strong natural urge to experiment and who revel in the rich workings of language, the verbal asceticism advocated by Hemingway and others can have a cramping, strait-jacketing effect.

In preceding chapters it has been seen how O'Faolain reacted to modern influences. The earliest stories were notable for their extravagant, unrestrained, sometimes uncontrollable imagery whose source was to be sought in the immediate and more distant past. *A Purse of Coppers* revealed a maturer, more aware writer. The stories in this collection gave evidence of an ability to compress both matter and language although acceptance of other models was never total.

Later, the extreme economy of language gave way to a manner which Maurice Harmon has called "deceptively artless and casual". A conversational, sometimes even colloquial style was adopted which successfully fused the essential with the seemingly superficial.

Yet employing a style which is not far removed from cliché has its own dangers. A writer like Somerset Maugham, with no great gift of language, found it difficult to rise above a certain level. T. O. Bancroft talks of Maugham as the "conscious artist of the cliché":

> If we turn from Somerset Maugham's theory to his practice we find that in his famous sentence about telling his stories after dinner he himself had really said the first and last word about his own art. He exemplifies to the full the advantages and the limitations of his chosen method. He carefully defines a group audience in rather a blunted frame of mind, which wants to be told something odd or striking, but is not ready to be upset or enter into subtleties . . . Thus you will find the narrator telling you that a man 'was grey with anguish'; that he 'forced a laugh to his shaking lips', he 'crumpled into a chair . . .' (*The Modest Art: A Survey of the Short Story in English*, London : Oxford University Press, 1968, p. 200).

Maugham openly admits his shortcomings :

> I knew that I had no lyrical quality. I had a small vocabulary and no efforts that I could make to enlarge it much availed me. I had little gift of metaphor . . .
> On the other hand, I had an acute power of observation, and it seemed to me that I could see a great many things that other people missed. I could put down in clear terms what I saw. I had a logical sense, and if no great feeling for the richness and strangeness of words, at all events a lively appreciation of their sound . . .
> On taking thought it seemed to me that I must aim at lucidity, simplicity and euphony. I have put these three qualities in the order of the importance I assigned to them. (*The Summing Up*, London : Penguin, 1963, p. 23).

For O'Faolain the problem was not so much of having no "lyrical quality" but of having too much, and of keeping it under control.

So far in this study, stories have been examined which are largely successful. In the present chapter an attempt will be made to show that three stories ("Lovers of the Lake", "The Trout", and "The Silence of the Valley"), written in the forties and fifties, are not as satisfactory as they might have been. The failure will be looked for at the language level. It will be argued that the language chosen for descriptive purposes is not always in harmony with what the story is about, or, that it is inappropriate to what is being described.

It will be helpful at this point to bear in mind comments made by two other writers :

> No matter how good a phrase or a simile he (the writer) may have if he puts it in where it is not absolutely necessary and ir-replaceable he is spoiling his work for egotism. Prose is architecture, not interior decoration, and the Baroque is over. (Ernest Hemingway, *Death in the Afternoon*, pp. 181-182).

> Anything, however slight, contains something that is still un-known. Let us find it. To describe a blazing fire or a tree in a plain, let us remain before that fire or that tree until it no longer looks to us like any other tree or any other fire. (Guy de Maupassant, *Pierre et Jean*, p. 13).

LANGUAGE LEVELS, NARRATIVE PERSPECTIVE, LOGIC

"The Trout" is a very tiny story. In four short pages the reader learns of an event in the life of a child. A little girl discovers a trout trapped in a pool of water. She creeps down at night to liberate the fish in the river. There are two immediate problems for a writer who is quite clearly narrating something which happened to his own daughter. How is he to control subjective feelings? How are the thoughts of the little girl to be presented? O'Faolain refers to these difficulties when he is discussing Chekhov whom he quotes :

> You may weep and moan over your stories, you may suffer with your characters, but it should be done in such a way that the reader does not detect it. The more objective, the stronger the impression. (*The Short Story*, p. 81).

O'Faolain attempts to resolve the difficulty by combining and blending. Sometimes it is third-person narrative, sometimes it is the mind of Julia which is reflected. The result is a somewhat uneasy, inconsistent mixture. At the centre, largely because of this blurred perspective, a mistake is made which more or less destroys the story. The child is shown kneeling on the ground looking at the fish :

> . . . they were both so excited that they were no longer afraid of the darkness as they hunched down and peered in at the fish pant-ing in his tiny prison, his silver stomach going up and down like an engine. ("The Trout", *Finest Stories*, p. 229).

Several mistakes, of logic or of fact, are made. It is dark in the tunnel under the bushes. Although the children might have been able to discern the fish, they would hardly have been able to make out its colour. Furthermore the colour is wrong. The stomach of a trout can be darkish brown, grey or yellow. In the gloom, and because the stomach is situated underneath the fish, the children would not have been able to see it at all. Possibly O'Faolain was thinking of the sides of the fish, in which case silver might have been acceptable.

The description is incorrect in other ways. Fish do not breathe like human beings. Water goes in through the mouth, comes out through the gills. The body does not move for respiratory purposes, so that the stomach could not have been "going up and down like an engine."

Why have these mistakes been made? Obviously O'Faolain has deliberately chosen imagery which is in harmony with what a child might feel. The word "panting" for example. Julia looks at the trout imprisoned in the tiny pool of water, its mouth constantly opening and closing. "Panting" implies breathlessness, fright, lack of oxygen. It is a word which might logically come to the mind of a child, so that it is right for her to repeat it to herself as the story proceeds. O'Faolain does not leave it at that. He later describes the fish's mechanical breathing process as "panting like an engine", personifying what is inanimate as he imagines a child would. Such apparent illogicality would be defensible if Julia were a different sort of person, or if she were imagining a fish and had not been looking directly at one. O'Faolain is contradicting himself too, in that he first says that it is the stomach, and not the mouth, whose functioning is like that of an engine.

Early on in the story the reader learns that Julia was "twelve, and at that age little girls are beginning to suspect most stories." Thus there is an unfortunate discrepancy between what O'Faolain intended and what the words express, resulting from the uncertain narrative viewpoint. Julia is not given to flights of fancy. She would therefore examine the fish carefully. She would see the mouth opening and closing. She could hardly fail to notice the movement of the gills.

In the phrase "panting like an engine" O'Faolain has given in to the temptation to introduce metaphor whose accuracy and appropriateness are belied by the facts and by the character of the person into whose mouth it is put. The adjective "silver" (applied to stomach) is objectionable for the same reason. It is a fairy-tale word which might be used by an adult in telling a traditional fable, or by a child who still believes in fairy-stories, but certainly not by

an observant, sceptical young girl who knows that there are "no
such things as fairy godmothers."

Another striking example of shifting language levels is to be found
later in the story :

> She sat up. Stephen was a hot lump of sleep, lazy thing. The
> Dark Walk would be full of little scraps of moon. She leapt up
> and looked out of the window, and somehow it was not so light-
> some now that she saw the dim mountains far away and the black
> firs against the breathing land and heard a dog say bark-bark.
> (TT, p. 230).

In this passage the uncertainty of narrative viewpoint is even more
clearly demonstrable. There is no reason why O'Faolain should not
have told the story in language reminiscent of fairy-tales. He could
equally well have seen the whole episode through the eyes and mind
of Julia. He attempts to incorporate both approaches, so that there
is no consistency of viewpoint. Julia is described as thinking of her
brother as "a hot lump of sleep, lazy thing". Would a child of twelve
use such an expression as "hot lump of sleep"? "Lazy thing", or
"Lazy lump", would be conceivable. In context, the expression does
not suggest a child looking at her sleeping brother, but somebody
writing about this, inventing a fanciful, slightly amusing image. This
suspicion is confirmed by what follows.

For example, "little scraps of moon" is hardly how Julia would
imagine the tunnel. It is dark by day. The light cast by the moon
would make the shadows even more terrifying at night. O'Faolain
is thinking purely in descriptive terms, looking at the scene with his
eyes and not – although this is the impression he wishes to convey –
through Julia's. He is losing the viewpoint in the metaphors.

As Julia looks through the window, she becomes aware of the
darkness outside; she sees the "dim" shape of the mountains and
the "black" outline of the trees. All this is what one would expect.
Yet O'Faolain brings in the words "lightsome" and "breathing";
once again changing the viewpoint from that of the girl to that of
the author. "Lightsome" is an archaism, a word one might find in a
traditional folk-tale, but it is not one which would pass through
Julia's mind. The same criticism may be levelled at "breathing". It is
a perfectly acceptable adjective in the sense that it suggests the living
quality of the countryside at night. But "breathing" is not a word
which would suggest itself to a child in such a situation. At the end
of the passage there is the curious phrase, "she . . . heard a dog say
bark-bark." "Say" implies baby-talk. It is almost the same as writing

"bow-wow". There need be no objection to the expression if it fulfils what the writer intends. But does it? Julia is looking out of the window, is becoming more and more aware of the eeriness of what lies outside.

Reference back to the barking of a dog on another occasion will make this point clearer :

> So we trudged on and every natural night sound terrified us, a bird's cry, a barking dog with his double note, bark-bark, and then silence, bark-bark, and like that now and again the whole night long from one mountainside or another. People say the most lonely thing of all at night is the bark of a dog at night . . . ("Fugue", *Finest Stories*, p. 36).

In the passage from "Fugue" the reference to the barking of a dog intensifies the sense of loneliness. Although O'Faolain presumably wished to bring home to the reader how frightening the dark garden was to Julia, by using the verb "say" in connection with a dog barking, he diminishes rather than heightens the tension. Instead of implying, by introducing the sound of the dog, that what lies outside is dangerous, or at the very least, intimidating, the insertion of a verb which acts as a distractor, has the opposite effect.

The result is that when Julia rushes out of the house, down into the tunnel, throws the trout into a jug so that she can put the fish back into the river, the tension is not genuine. In spite of verbs like "flurried", phrases such as "mad with fright", "her teeth ground", – slightly humorous, possibly deliberately cliché expressions, representing the author's attitude – the reader will not be able to take the situation of the girl seriously. Of course there is no danger. But that is not the point. It is an adventure for the girl to go out into the garden at night. The sense of real anxiety is not maintained because the writer does not keep his verbal camera unswervingly pointed at the girl.

EXTERNAL APPEARANCES

If a writer of prose knows enough about what he is writing about he may omit things that he knows and the reader, if the writer is writing truly enough, will have a feeling of those things as strongly as though the writer had stated them. (Ernest Hemingway, *Death in the Afternoon*, p. 182).

The writer of short stories in the twentieth century is faced with many technical difficulties; not least, the necessity of creating his own artistic shorthand. There is no space for portraiture. Dabs of the impressionist's brush are called for. The writer must somehow make what has been called "pictorial contact". A direct or indirect connection between a person's appearance and what a story is about should be ascertainable. Otherwise physical description is irrelevant, or may even have the unwanted function of distracting or detracting. In most of the stories so far discussed in this study, reasons were found for the inclusion of physical description.

Many of O'Faolain's stories are written round some central idea. Everything in the story must have the quality of contributing to the clarifying and strengthening of that idea. Yet there are stories in which physical description occurs but where the necessity for such description, or even for the inclusion of certain characters must be questioned. It will be argued that such a conclusion may be drawn in part from the kind of language used to present such characters. Certain sections of "The Silence of the Valley" will be examined in an attempt to show that indulgence in metaphor can lead to a lack of clarity, even to illogicality.

The story is about a group of tourists staying at a country hotel at a time when the last of the great Irish story-tellers dies. These outsiders are placed against a background of great natural beauty.

They are introduced as follows :

> There were five of them, all looking out the door at the lake . . .
> Behind the counter was an American soldier, blond, blankly handsome, his wide-vision glasses convexing the sky against his face. Leaning against the counter was a priest, jovial, fat, ruddy, his Roman collar off and his trousers stuck into his socks – he had been up the mountain all day rough-shooting. Leaning against the pink-washed wall was a dark young man with pince-nez; he had the smoldering ill-disposed eyes of the incorrigible Celt – "always eager to take offence," as the fourth of the party had privately cracked. She was a sturdy, red-mopped young woman in blue slacks now sitting on the counter drinking whiskey. She sometimes seemed not at all beantiful, and sometimes her heavy features seemed to have a strong beauty of their own, for she was on a hair trigger between a glowering Beethoven and "The Laughing Cavalier". Sometimes her mouth was broody; suddenly it would expand into a half-batty gaiety. Her deep-set eyes ran from gloom to irony, to challenge, to wild humor. She had severe eyebrows that floated as gently as a veil in the wind. She was a Scot. The fifth of the group was a sack of a man, a big fat school inspector, also with his collar off. He had cute ingratiating eyes. ("The Silence of the Valley", *FS*, pp. 246–247).

Robert H. Hopkins interprets this story as a moving lament for a world which has died :

> Ireland is portrayed as perhaps the last citadel of a folk-world tradition in Western culture that is slowly being destroyed by the pressures and complexities of a civilization based on urban life, technology, and power. ("The Pastoral Mode of Sean O'Faolain's 'The Silence of the Valley' ", *Studies in Short Fiction*, 1963–64, Vol. 1, Number 1, p. 93).

Hopkins provides illuminating explanations for many seemingly superficial happenings and symbols – for example, the eel-fishing – which he often traces back to Celtic mythology. Hopkins ranks the tourists ". . . according to the degree to which they have departed from the kingdom of nature", in the order : the American soldier, the Scots girl, the inspector of schools, and the priest. They are types, and are presented as such. This using of types is legitimate, particularly since O'Faolain clearly wishes to make fun, for example, of the "incorrigible Celt".

He is not satisfied to leave it at that. O'Faolain finds it necessary to qualify these individuals further; sometimes by personal reference, sometimes by offering additional, though not essential information, adopting descriptive terms whose appropriateness must on occasion be challenged.

None of these characters is individually important to the story. They are representatives of a decadent, modern world. They are useful as a contrast to what may be seen all round them : the quiet, unchanging beauty of nature in which the old Irish story-teller had his home. For that reason it is essential that they be presented briefly and anonymously, with no details which might attract unnecessary attention.

The American, for example, is introduced in this way. His eyes are concealed behind sun-glasses, and he is described as "blankly handsome".

The same is true of the priest who is characterised with three adjectives : "jovial, fat, ruddy". It will be remembered that the majority of O'Faolain's priests incline to corpulence.

The other young man is also characterised in very few words, although the fact that he is bad-tempered is mentioned twice : ". . . he had the smoldering ill-disposed eyes of the incorrigible Celt – 'always eager to take offence,' as the fourth member of the party had privately cracked."

Only two aspects of the inspector's appearance are mentioned : his corpulence and his eyes. These physical attributes are repeated.

I

The inspector is "a sack of a man"; he is also "big fat". The priest too, has been introduced with the adjective "fat", but perhaps this repetition is further evidence that O'Faolain is "type-casting".

However the combination "cute, ingratiating" in connection with the inspector's eyes is questionable. The expression "ingratiating eyes" would make sense. The addition of "cute", a slang American-ism, is too imprecise to be understandable. The two adjectives are contradictory in that "cute" at least suggests something positive, whereas "ingratiating" is negative in implication.

Nearly two paragraphs are devoted to the Scots girl. She is one of the group at the hotel, neither more nor less important than the others, yet she is described at considerable length. One might ask why O'Faolain finds it necessary to say more than, "she was a sturdy, red-mopped young woman in blue slacks", particularly since much of what follows is not easily understandable. It is certainly not a passage in which the writer is thinking of the contact between "eye and object, between object and reader".

Again there is a blending of formal with colloquial English which does little to add to the clarity of the description. O'Faolain looks at the girl's face in order to interpret from this what he feels her character to be, "sometimes her mouth was broody; sometimes it would expand into a half-batty gaiety". Presumably the young woman was impetuous, temperamental. This, one may assume from other sections of the passage. O'Faolain is attempting to achieve an effect which cannot be realised through words such as "broody" or the phrase "expand into a half-batty gaiety". The impossibility becomes apparent if one tries to imagine what the girl's mouth would look like if her mouth behaved in the manner suggested.

The writer has an idea or an object which he wishes to augment in verbal terms. Metaphor takes over, to confuse, even obliterate. This process is most clearly demonstrated in the sentence : "She had severe eyebrows that floated as gently as a veil in the wind.". O'Faolain makes a statement ("She had severe eyebrows . . .") which he attempts to intensify by adding a simile which is both contradic-tory and void of meaning. Although it is not really necessary to know what kind of eyebrows the girl had, the expression "severe eyebrows" provides enough information for the reader to imagine for himself what they looked like. The additional image, in O'Faolain's own words is "part of the attempt to carry on and expand the effect after the sense has been given."

This is a central problem for O'Faolain all through his writing career, a problem which he never completely overcomes. He has himself analysed and defined what happens :

... the writer who luxuriates goes on with the echoes of his first image of idea. His emotions and his thoughts dilate, the style dilates with them, and in the end he is trying to write a kind of verbal music to convey feelings that the mere sense of the words cannot give. He is chasing the inexpressible. (*FS*, p. vii).

Just how far the "echoes" may take a writer can be further exemplified in "The Silence of the Valley" :

> One clear star above the mountain wall gleamed. Seeing it her eyebrows floated upwards softly for sheer joy. "Yes," she said quietly, "it will be another grand day – tomorrow." And her eyebrows sank, very slowly, like a falling curtain. (SOV, p. 265).

O'Faolain obviously wants to emphasize the fact that the Scottish girl was visibly moved by the beauty of what she saw through the window. His aim should be to use the girl to bring home to the reader a sense of the loveliness of the valley in the evening. Instead the reader is left with a strange mental picture of the girl. Eyebrows cannot "float" or "fall". Perhaps O'Faolain was thinking of eyelashes. The "falling curtain" simile might then have worked.

There is one more word in the last section which needs to be considered. "Seeing it her eyebrows floated upwards softly for sheer joy." What meaning can "softly" have? Raising eyebrows is never a noisy action. Once again a metaphorical situation has got out of hand.

One sentence in the first description of the girl has wider implications. The Scots girl is said "to be on a hairtrigger between a glowering Beethoven and The Laughing Cavalier". Hopkins suggests that the girl is supposed to be a "modern, masculine type of woman". As evidence he cites the fact that she smokes Panatellas, her "sturdy" build, "blue slacks" and her concern with birth control. This may be the reason why O'Faolain compares her with male models. Later he takes up the same metaphors, echoing the first: "Her face gathered, ceased to be 'The Laughing Cavalier' and became Beethoven in labor." (p. 250).

The "Beethoven in labor" metaphor is perhaps amusing. All that O'Faolain is saying is that the expression on the girl's face changed from amusement to anger. Furthermore it is only possible for the reader to deduce that if he knows the two models on which O'Faolain is drawing. In this particular instance it is likely that most readers will have seen reproductions of "The Laughing Cavalier" or portraits of Beethoven. Yet doubts must still remain as to the effectiveness, or even desirability, of using such models for descriptive purposes.

The real danger occurs when models are chosen which will be known only to a very limited number of readers, possibly only to the writer himself. In such a case, the author is writing solely for himself.

For example in a later story, "A Sweet Colleen", the two main male characters see the girl they love in terms of pictures at the National Gallery where the girl works. O'Faolain knows the pictures, as do the two men, but the reader, unless he takes the trouble to go to the National Gallery will not, so that allusions to Rossetti, High Renaissance, Veneziano, Pollaiuolo, and Botticelli are quite lost on him.

The Scottish girl in "The Silence of the Valley" is a minor character, so that indulgence in fanciful, strained, or wholly inaccurate imagery will not destroy the effect of the story completely. However, if inaccurate metaphor is applied to characters who matter, or whose situation is, or is potentially, tragic, then the success of a story cannot fail to be diminished. The widow in "The Silence of the Valley" is introduced as follows :

> She was a tiny aged woman who looked as if her whole body from scalp to soles was wrinkled and yellow; her face, her bare arms, her bare chest were as golden as a dried apple; even her eyeballs seemed wrinkled. But her white hair flowed upward all about her like a Fury in magnificent wild snakes from under an old fisherman's tweed hat, and her mobile mouth and her loud – too loud – voice gave out a tremendous vitality. When she was a young girl she must have been as lively as a minnow in a mountain stream. (SOV, p. 252).

As in the description of the Scottish girl, there is a constant striving for more and more effect. The passage begins with a statement of fact : "She was a tiny aged woman . . ." Instead of just saying that the woman's skin was wrinkled, the writer attempts to intensify the impression by suggesting that the woman's body "looked as if her whole body from scalp to soles was wrinkled and yellow . . ." This idea is continued in the next sentence, although here, the writer begins to lose control : ". . . her face, her bare arms, her bare chest were as golden as a dried apple; even her eyeballs seemed wrinkled." The woman's skin has been described as "yellow" and "wrinkled". Now one is asked to believe that it is as "golden" as a "dried apple". "Golden" suggests shining, glowing, so that the first image is contradicted by the second. "Golden" also implies other qualities and is a much less accurate word than yellow.

The process is continued in the sentences which follow. It is not enough for the hair to "flow upward", it must become "wild snakes". Since the woman is wearing a hat, it becomes difficult to imagine exactly how this happens. The woman's uncombed hair merely sticks out from under the hat. Similarly, in her youth, the woman is not only compared with "a minnow", it is a "minnow in a mountain stream", which is an attempt to strengthen one cliché by adding another.

Just what has happened may be more easily understood if a section from a story ("The End of the Record") is quoted in which another old woman – almost certainly the same woman – is introduced :

> She did not appear to see them. She was humming happily to herself. Her bony fingers were wound about an ancient rosary beads. Her white hair floated up above a face as tiny and wrinkled as a forgotten crab apple. All her teeth were gone so that her face was as broad as it was long : it was as if the midwife had pressed the baby's chin between thumb and forefinger. The doctor gently laid his hand under the tiny chin and turned her face towards him. (*FS*, p. 267).

It is striking in this passage that the imagery – although many of the same words are used as in the first description – gradually fills in the lines and wrinkles of a face which the reader can imagine for himself. The series of similes have a direct and clear connection with what the writer wishes the reader to envisage. Even the verbs are modified. The hair does not "flow upward", it "floats".

The words are applied in such a way that a successful combination of clarity with illustrative metaphor is achieved. For example, the woman's face this time is not presented in the contradictory phrase : "as golden as a dried apple". Instead it is "as tiny and wrinkled as a forgotten crab apple.". Both shape and appearance of the face are included in the comparison. The apple is qualified. It is a "forgotten crab apple".

The aptness of the word "forgotten" will be better appreciated if it is considered in context. The old woman, whose mind has gone, is herself forgotten. She lives in a hospital for the old. Thus the adjective "forgotten" goes on working at other levels, brilliantly stressing the old woman's situation. The contours of the face are carefully, accurately depicted in simple, visual terms so that there is no blurring, no false association.

If one returns to the first description of the old woman now, one might be tempted to find another explanation for the exaggerated metaphor. Many of the descriptive terms are cliché : for example, the comparison of the woman's face with an apple, "fury in magnificent wild snakes", "mobile mouth", "lively as a minnow". Is it not possible that the straining for effect may have come about as a result of the attempt to put new life into old metaphor.

There are other dangers for the writer who permits metaphor to brush logic and clarity aside. It is quite possible that if a writer is thinking of an effect he will forget the object of his description. For example, when the widow goes upstairs :

She lumbered up the ladderlike stairs . . . They lumbered down the steep stairs. (SOV, pp. 252–253).

The widow was introduced as "a tiny aged woman", so that "lumbered" is inappropriate since it conveys an impression which is incorrect. On the other hand when she and the priest come down the stairs, the priest's movements may be indicated by the use of the verb "to lumber" since he is a fat and clumsy man.

Mistakes of this kind have already been commented on in "The Trout". Errors of a slightly different nature, although resulting from a desire to create an effect, are to be found in "Lovers of the Lake".

After completing several rounds of prayer on the island in bare feet, Jenny's toe, knee and ankle are bleeding. Bobbie says : "I may tell you that my feet are in such a condition I won't be able to play golf for a week." ("Lovers of the Lake", FS, p. 325). Yet on the day the pilgrimage ends, Bobbie goes fishing for most of the afternoon. Later that same night they dance until three o'clock.

One of the most unfortunate results of exaggerated metaphor is that a very different reaction may be provoked from what was intended. Because the writer does not control his imagery, the reader will be left with a number of alternatives to choose from, or, if a metaphor is totally dissociative, the reader will think only of the metaphor and not of the object to which it is being applied.

In "Lovers of the Lake" a young woman speaks to Jenny at the end of one of the circuits. The young woman is twenty-four, has had six children in as many years. She loves her husband but is terrified at the thought of continuing to have a child every year.

She wore a scarlet beret. She was smoking again. She began to talk and the talk flowed from her without stop. She had fine broad shoulders, a big mobile mouth, and a pair of wild goat's eyes. After a while it became clear that the woman was beside herself with terror. (LOL, p. 327).

Only three details of physical appearance are given : shoulders,

mouth, eyes, the kind of impression which one might gain on
casually looking at a person one does not know. Yet once again a
mouth is referred to as being "mobile" (the same adjective was used
to describe the widow's mouth in "The Silence of the Valley"). It is
a cliché word which has no clear meaning. The young woman has
"wild goat's eyes" : presumably referring to the wide staring appearance of the eyes of a goat. The adjective "wild" is added to emphasize the girl's terror.

Yet is the description really necessary at all? The girl is just an
anonymous figure in the crowd. She is part of that background of
human insufficiency in which Jenny finds herself and against which
she measures herself. It is not the girl's appearance which matters,
but what the girl stands for. Furthermore the reader learns at the
end of the passage that "the woman was beside herself with terror".
The three descriptive phrases, particularly the expression "goat's
eyes", have a distractive quality.

O'Faolain returns again and again to the eyes, referring to the girl
later in the story as "Goat's Eyes", a synecdoche which in context
seems insensitive. There is a difference between saying that someone
has goat's eyes, implying that that person is frightened, and calling
somebody "Goat's Eyes". The reader may be amused, whereas the
writer's original intention was to provoke sympathy.

In another place, O'Faolain employs the same metaphor to suggest
two emotions :

> The two goat's eyes dilated with fear and joy. Her hands shook
> like a drunkard's. (LOL, p. 327).

The girl is terrified of the priest, but simultaneously aroused at
the thought of her husband. O'Faolain attempts to reproduce this
double emotion in the girl's eyes. It is certainly reasonable to assume
that fear may be expressed in the staring look of a goat's eyes. It is
more than doubtful if it is permissible to suggest the opposite emotion
by employing the same metaphor.

Elsewhere O'Faolain demonstrates far greater control :

> . . . his (Hanafan's) eyes dilated under his black hat with the image
> of his memory. His eyes were not cranky now, but soft and big.
> ("Admiring the Scenery", FS, p. 108).

The writer's eye is keenly fixed on Hanafan and the problem
which he wishes to illuminate. There is no distractive metaphor.
Something of the same confusion, of disintegrated effect, may be

found elsewhere. For example, the passage in which Julia runs through the dark tunnel beneath the bushes :

> For the first few yards she always had the memory of the sun behind her, then she felt the dusk closing swiftly down on her so that she screamed with pleasure and raced on to reach the light at the far end; and it was always just a little too long in coming so that she emerged gasping, clasping her hands, laughing, drinking in the sun. When she was filled with heat and glare she would turn and consider the ordeal again. ("The Trout", p. 228).

Obviously O'Faolain is not being serious here, so that the reader's surprise at finding the word "ordeal" at the end of a passage in which a pleasurable experience has been presented is tempered by the realisation that O'Faolain has his tongue in his cheek. Yet O'Faolain is still somewhat caught between amusement at the girl's behaviour, the attempt to re-create this in words, and the temptation to let the metaphor build up the action into something much bigger than it really is.

Small inaccuracies and straining for effect weaken the force of the passage. Would the girl be likely to emerge from the tunnel "clasping" her hands? She might have her fists clenched to indicate tension. If she had her hands clasped together – which is what the word suggests – she would very easily fall over. Instead of saying that Julia thought about running through the tunnel again after she had got her breath back, O'Faolain brings in the fanciful phrase : "When she was filled with heat and glare" as if the fact that she was warm affected her decision to "consider the ordeal again".

A further problem arising from the description of external appearance may be exemplified from "Lovers of the Lake". Jenny and Bobby are travelling to Lough Derg in the car. Jenny looks at her lover :

> She looked sideways, with amusement, at his ruddy, healthy, hockey-player face, glummering under the peak of his checked cap. The brushes at his temple were getting white. Everything about him bespoke the distinguished Dublin surgeon on holiday : his pale-green shirt, his darker-green tie, his double-breasted waistcoat, his driving-gloves with the palms made of woven cord. (LOL, p. 311).

The suggestion is that what Bobby is wearing is indicative of his profession. Is one to assume that all Dublin surgeons dress like this when holidaying? That Bobby is a doctor is of interest, but that he wears this particular kind of clothing is irrelevant to the story.

It will be remembered that in "Up the Bare Stairs" the narrator looks across the carriage at the man opposite him, tries from what he sees to guess the man's nationality and profession. The narrator's guess is wrong, but there was a reason for O'Faolain to begin the story in this way and for such minute description of the stranger's clothes and general appearance.

There is also inconsistency in the language used in the quotation. The description reflects the thoughts of Jenny. Hence the adoption of expressions such as "glummering", "hockey-player". Yet words like "brushes" or "bespoke" suggest that it is the writer who is taking up the narration again.

The problem may be further illustrated by looking at another example. While driving to Lough Derg, Bobby and Jenny ("Lovers of the Lake") have a long argument. An explosion of temper on the part of Bobby is presented as follows :

> Their speed shot up at once to sixty-five. He drove through Bundoran's siesta hour like the Chariot of the Apocalypse. (p. 313).

A speed of sixty-five mph would not strike the driver of today as being particularly fast, so that the cumulative effect of the expressions "Bundoran's siesta hour" and "Chariot of the Apocalypse" is diminished. It is perfectly clear from what he says that Bobby is infuriated by Jenny's announcement that she intends to do the pilgrimage. Additional indications of his annoyance are superfluous.

NATURE : SETTING

One might go on from what was discussed in the previous section to make the assertion that the appearance of cliché is an indication that something irrelevant has come into the story, or that a certain loss of control on the part of the writer has occurred.

It was noticed for example in characterisations of the tourists and of the widow in "The Silence of the Valley" that criticism could be made of the metaphors, language, sometimes even of logic. These lapses are all the more striking for appearing beside passages of great beauty. For example, the first paragraph :

> Only in the one or two farmhouses about the lake, or in the fishing hotel at its edge – preoccupations of work and pleasure – does one ever forget the silence of the valley. Even in the winter, when the great cataracts slide down the mountain face, the echoes

J

of falling water are fitful : the winds fetch and carry them. In the summer a fisherman will hear the tinkle of the ghost of one of those falls only if he steals among the mirrored reeds under the pent of the cliff, and withholds the plash of his oars. These tiny muted sounds will awe and delight him by the vacancy out of which they creep, intermittently. (SOV, p. 246).

The echoes of this opening section go on sounding right through to the end of the story. The natural silence of the lake reflects the death of the old man whose voice has been stilled for ever. The beauty of the landscape remains, but it is mute, appealing only through its outward appearance.

As in "Lady Lucifer", O'Faolain manages to convey a mediate view of nature. If there is beauty, it is a beauty which is in the eye of the beholder. It is not animate. While the death of the old man, and with him of a whole tradition of story-telling, is tragic, showing this by means of reproducing the beautiful natural surroundings in which he passed his life is not permitted to reveal direct personal involvement of the writer. The effect on the reader may be moving, but it will have been achieved because the reader becomes aware, through contemplating nature, of what has passed away. Like the tourists, he is but a casual traveller to the country who, when his visit is over, will turn his back on what he came to see.

The title of the story, repeated in the introduction, makes clear that nature is mute. The irrevocable break between man and nature is implicit from the start. Only in the farmhouses near the lake or in the fishing hotel is it possible to escape from the silence. Only in the company of his own kind, and in surroundings he has made, can man communicate. The sense of depersonalisation deepens as the paragraph continues. It is even intensified by the personifications of nature : for example, when the winds are described as fetching and carrying the echoes. They are echoes of something which is no longer there. The echo effect is carried on to the end where there is the revealing sentence : "These tiny muted sounds will awe and delight him by the vacancy out of which they creep, intermittently." The sounds come from "a vacancy". No identifiable person is brought into the first paragraph. There is merely mention of an anonymous fisherman. The personal note is completely excluded, so that the sense of a void is maintained right through. One is reminded of the ending of a later story :

I wished I was down where the bright lights of the empty esplanades glinted in the calm, the whispering, the indifferent sea. ("The Human Thing", *The Heat of the Sun*, p. 99).

There is metaphor in the passage from "The Silence of the Valley", but the words are so chosen that a visual, sometimes audible, effect is created. Even where powerful words are employed, these can be justified. For example, "great cataracts slide down the mountain face." After winter rains, the small mountain streams overflow so that sheets of water come down the mountainside. From a distance – it is stressed that even in winter the sound does not carry – they would appear to "slide" rather than flow. O'Faolain says that the muted sounds "awe and delight". The word "awe" must have been put in deliberately, because the fisherman will feel he is in the presence of something which he does not understand yet which commands his respect.

Even where poetic or archaic words occur (for example, "pent" for steep slope, "plash" for splash) they do not lead to the introduction of false emotion or any blurring of the visual and audible impression. "Plash" for example probably more accurately reflects the kind of sound O'Faolain wished to intimate, since it suggests a quieter noise than splash.

Elsewhere in "The Silence of the Valley", the descriptive passages go on echoing the "ghosts" of sound, constantly, though not insistently, drawing attention to the slow-moving, almost static quality of life in this remote valley :

> They all turned to watch the frieze of small black cows passing slowly before the scalloped water, the fawny froth, the wall of mountain. (SOV, p. 249).

> The morning was a blaze of colour. The island was a floating red flower. The rhododendrons around the edges of the island were replicated in the smooth lee water which they barely touched. (SOV, p. 260).

The metaphors in these two passages give greater force to the visual impression. They do not have vague emotional appeal. Where, for example, the reader might not understand if the metaphor were left by itself, O'Faolain explains. The reader is told what O'Faolain means by "a floating red flower". The employment of words like "frieze" and "scalloped" stops all sense of movement. The water and the animals are seen from a distance, their outline is petrified on the page.

There are occasions in the story when O'Faolain eschews metaphor completely, letting the actions of characters, seen against an appropriate background become self-explanatory. For example, O'Faolain deliberately, and quite rightly, avoids bathos in his description of the actual burial. He is at pains to stress that the widow does not give way immediately to her grief. He has her laugh and talk with visitors, constantly referring to the man who has died. Yet the story is about tragedy, although the tragedy is not the death of the cobbler. That is sad, but it is an expected end, the termination of a long life. O'Faolain rightly plays this down. Only when the coffin is about to be covered, does the old woman break down :

> Nobody else made a sound until the first shovel of earth struck the brass plate on the lid and then the widow, defeated at last, cried out without restraint. As the earth began to fall more softly her wailing became more quiet. (SOV, p. 264).

There is striking concord between what is happening and the reactions of a main character. The old woman's weeping is balanced against the sound of earth falling first loudly on the coffin, afterwards more quietly into the ground. There is no imagery and only one verb which does more than reproduce the actions of those present at the burial. The widow is "defeated at last", she lets her tears flow. Here the verbal camera is perfectly focused. No extraneous metaphor is permitted to come between the reader and what the writer intends him to see. O'Faolain becomes a part of the "creatures of his invention", so that although what they do is dictated by him, yet their actions are natural and comprehensible in terms of what they have become on the pages of the story.

Unfortunately, consistent harmony of metaphor with the central idea is not maintained all the way through, as may be seen from the concluding section of the story :

> The red-haired girl leaned to the window and shaded her eyes against the pane. She could see how the moon touched the trees on the island with a ghostly tenderness. One clear star above the mountain wall gleamed. Seeing it her eyebrows floated upward softly for sheer joy.
> "Yes," she said quietly, "it will be another grand day tomorrow."
> And her eyebrows sank, very slowly, like a falling curtain. (SOV, p. 265).

The description of the girl has been discussed earlier in the chapter. It is perhaps now possible to find reasons for what has gone wrong. Throughout the story nature has been depicted as part of a world with which modern man no longer has any personal contact. Nature has been used as a reflector of emptiness, as a medium for passing on echoes which are meaningless to modern man and which his ears are hardly capable of registering at all.

The girl has been shown as a masculine type who is very unemotional. Suddenly at the end she is portrayed as succumbing, almost swooning at the sight of moonlight on the water. This is not a logical reaction. It will be remembered how the doctor responds at the end of "Lady Lucifer". He shows his appreciation of the beauty which he sees all around him. Unlike his two companions, he is not a dreamer so that while taking from the evening landscape a sense of its loveliness, he does not indulge in foolish meditations on what might have been.

The girl is not important in the story, except in a secondary function as representative of a degenerate modern society. The death of the old man, the passing away of an age-old tradition, the widow's reactions, placed against the backdrop of impersonal nature, are the heart of the story. ". . . the moon touched the trees on the island with a ghostly tenderness." The introduction of traditional, clichéd associations of nature breaks the clarity of line, diminishes the effectiveness of the story, particularly when one thinks back to the powerful restraint of the opening lines.

An interesting parallel to the end of "The Silence of the Valley" may be found in the last sentences of "Lovers of the Lake" :

> They leaned on the railing and he put his arm about her waist, and she put hers around his, and they gazed at the moon silently raking its path across the sea towards Aran. (LOL, p. 336).

There can be no objection to the language used in the passage. Yet such descriptions of two lovers standing arm in arm looking up at the moon have appeared in countless poems, novels, plays and stories. It is of course possible that the lovers would have behaved as O'Faolain suggests, but doubts must remain as to the desirability of choosing such a hackneyed ending.

"Lovers of the Lake" is the story of two middle-aged people who have reached a crisis in their relationship. In desperation, the woman decides to go on a pilgrimage.

Although they pass through nature to reach their destination, nature has no influence on the course of the story. Isolation, meditation, fasting, bring both main characters to a realisation of what they are personally, and of what they mean to each other. Neither of them is religious, so that they can find no solace in faith.

O'Faolain offers no solutions while revealing through the two main characters man's essential loneliness and self-concern :

. . . she was overcome by the thought that inside ourselves we have no room without a secret door; no solid self that has not a ghost inside it trying to escape. If I leave Bobby I still have George. If I leave George I still have myself ... (LOL, p. 329).

They were close, their shoulders touched, but between them there stood that impenetrable wall of identity that segregates every human being in a private world of self. Feeling it she realised at last that it is only in such places like the lake-island that the barriers of self break down . . . Only when love desires nothing but renunciation, total surrender, does self surpass self. (LOL, pp. 330–331).

Jenny has not found God on the island, but she has realised her limitations. The two lovers have come closer to finally understanding that life only has meaning if they live in and through each other, even if they will never marry, never have children.

When this awareness comes to them the story is over but, presumably because of a pre-conceived time-scheme, the remaining hours of the fast are related, the long drive afterwards to the hotel where after midnight they eat, drink, dance, sleep.

There is no need for the long final section. The central problem has been exhaustively dealt with already. The reader has long since learned that Jenny and Bobby are both attracted by material things. Jenny says : "I admit that I like the things of the flesh." It is a positive quality of the story that O'Faolain makes no attempt to hide human weaknesses and frailty. There can therefore be nothing new for the reader to learn about these two characters by watching them eat, drink and make merry.

The very fact that they are unnecessary may help to explain why the concluding paragraphs are unsatisfactory.

These homing twelve o'clockers from Lough Derg are well known in every hotel all over the west of Ireland. Revelry is the reward of penance. The porter welcomed them as if they were heroes returned from a war . . . he assured them that the ritual grill was at the moment sizzling over the fire, he proffered them hot baths, and he told them where to discover the bar . . . They had to win a corner of the counter . . . After supper they relished the bar once more. (LOL, p. 335).

The tone of the narration has suddenly changed. From speaking through his two main characters, or writing in the third-person, O'Faolain makes the section quoted sound like a travelogue ("These homing twelve o'clockers from Lough Derg are well known . . .) as if he were addressing his public through the medium of a tabloid.

There is a very perceptible break in the story at this point. No doubt O'Faolain wished to show the two lovers coming in from the cold, returning to more normal habits of self-indulgence. Instead of standing out, they are swallowed up in the crowd. It is conceivable that O'Faolain intended the language, through the adoption of cliché and journalese, to make subtle commentary on what the lives of these people amount to. Yet there is no real evidence of irony.

Only occasionally do the cliché expressions come from the porter's mouth. It is not the porter who says, "Revelry is the reward of penance", "heroes returned from a war". It is difficult to imagine what gain there is in using "assured" for told, "proffer" for offer, "discover" for find, "win a corner" for get a seat, "relished" for enjoyed.

This section leads on to the final scene where Bobby and Jenny stare arm in arm at the moon which is moving in the direction, not of just any island, but of Aran, itself the object of sentimental association.

Neither Bobby nor Jenny has any connection with the countryside. They are city-dwellers who find themselves on an island for the period of the pilgrimage. It must therefore be doubted whether there can be any justification for presenting, or attempting to present, emotional problems in terms of nature, or of metaphor which is expressed through natural phenomena. Where there is no connection, and links with nature are introduced artificially, that artificiality can express itself through inaccurate or false metaphor. For example, when Jenny and Bobby are in the middle of an argument, there comes the following : "A sea gull moaned high overhead." (LOL, p. 313). The word "moaned" was probably inserted for humorous effect. However the row between Jenny and Bobby is anything but light-hearted, so that instead of intensifying, the metaphor distracts by switching attention from what it is supposed to emphasize. Elsewhere :

A slow rift in the clouds let down a star; by its light she saw his smile. (LOL, p. 320).

The moon touched a black window with colour. (LOL, p. 322).

Here the mountains walled in the bogland plain with cobalt air – in the fading light the land was losing all solidity. Clouds like soapsuds rose and rose over the edges of the mountains until they glowed as if there was a fire of embers behind the blue ranges. (LOL, p. 333).

It is a fanciful image to say that a star is "let down" by a break in

the cloud. In this case "star" is being used to project the same association as moon, suggesting something of great significance to lovers.
A star, one star, could hardly cast enough light for Jenny to see the
expression on her lover's face. Can the moon "touch a black window
with colour"? The moon, emerging from behind cloud, might make
a window visible. The light would not be strong enough to reveal
colour.

The third quotation comes from that part of the story in which the
lovers travel from the island to their hotel, and where the story is
already over. This description of nature is successful in that it is
possible to visualise the details of the sky from what the words say.
Yet the simile "clouds like soapsuds", while accurate in what it expresses, has other, ludicrous associations, so that the imagery once
more acts as a distractor.

Perhaps this would be an appropriate moment to quote a remark
O'Faolain makes of a story by Henry James :

> All I would excise are some prolixities amounting to repetition;
> the 'cutting' process which any writer may legitimately do after
> his first draft. (*The Short Story*, p. 213).

VERBAL AND ADVERBIAL CONSTRUCTIONS

For a century the novel had staggered along under the weight
of a colossal convention of fancy mechanics in the matter of
dialogue. The novel had managed somehow to survive it; the short
story had been in constant danger of collapsing. In this convention the words of a character had their intonation, flavour, emotion, or meaning underlined by the writer. Thus : "He reiterated
with a manifest show of anger"; "she ventured to remark with a
melancholy intonation in her voice"; "he declared haltingly"; "he
stammered out in frightened accents"; "he interposed"; "he inter-
jected with a low laugh", and so on and so on. Wads of this verbal
padding bolstered up the conversation of every novel from Dickens
down to the fourpenny paperback. (H. E. Bates, *The Modern
Short Story*, pp. 171–172).

In his successful stories O'Faolain generally avoids such primitive
techniques. Yet in some of the longer pieces in the early and later
work there are lapses. For example in the stories being examined in
this chapter :

> They heard him in quizzical boredom. (SOV, p. 247).
> They applauded perfunctorily. (SOV, p. 247).

The priest intervened diplomatically . . . (SOV, p. 249).

The young woman . . . threw back her whiskey delightedly. (SOV, p. 249).

He replied amiably . . . (LOL, p. 310).

. . . he looked at her peeringly. (LOL, p. 310).

. . . she lowered her head appealingly . . . (LOL, p. 310).

She . . . kissed him sedately . . . (LOL, p. 311).
She looked pensively . . . (LOL, p. 311).

Characters tend to laugh, groan, gesticulate wildly, and their features contort grotesquely as the writer labours to make clear what is often unmistakable. The result can be irrelevance, distraction from what is important, even inaccuracy :

She had severe eyebrows that floated as gently as a veil in the wind. (SOV, p. 247).

Her face gathered, ceased to be "The Laughing Cavalier" and became Beethoven in labor. (SOV, p. 250).

She broke into peals of laughter. (SOV, p. 254).

She groaned comically . . . (SOV, p. 254).

. . . she wagged her flaming head warningly and made eyes of mock horror . . . (SOV, p. 255).

. . . her mouth rolling the lipstick into her lips; her eyes rolling around the mirror. (LOL, p. 315).

She slewed her head swiftly away from his angry eyes . . .

She slewed back to him. He slewed away to look up the long, empty road before them. He slewed back; he made as if to speak; he slewed away impatiently again. (LOL, p. 314).

In a later story even greater concentrations of such devices may occur. O'Faolain is attempting to be humorous :

. . . he says, with a lewd wink.

. . . she upbraided.

. . . and he winked at us again

. . . she begged.

. . . I said, friendly-like, . . .

. . . Olly grinned.

. . . Olly grinned a No to all of them.

. . . He clicked his tongue and raised shocked eyebrows.

. . . she grimaced.

. . . he gestured.

. . . she said and glared at him.

. . . She was chuckling. Olly finished his yarn, winked at me, and looked expectantly at Janey. Her face at once did a quick curtain and she said severely :
  'Oliver !'
He guffawed. His gooseberry eyes rolled in their sockets. He guffawed.

. . . Janey Anne gurgled. Olly finished, winked, waited, got his 'Oliver !' and guffawed happily.
  ("One Man, One Boat, One Girl", *The Heat of the Sun*, pp. 106–107).

Sometimes the natural word order is changed; or transitive verbs are made to work intransitively :

. . . soothed the school inspector. (SOV, p. 247).

. . . yielded the Celt. (SOV, p. 247).

. . . reprimanded the Celt. (SOV, p. 249).

. . . she accused. (TT, p. 229).

Nearly all these examples are to be found directly after statements which are self-explanatory, so that nothing is added to the sense by such verbal or adverbial constructions.

On occasion O'Faolain invents adverbs, or employs adverbs in unusual combinations :

. . . she wagged her flaming head warningly . . . (SOV, p. 255).

The offal glistened oilily. (SOV, p, 256).

Once the American chased her laughingly . . . (SOV, p. 257).

The lake crawled livingly . . . (SOV, p. 258).

. . . the coffin . . . was laid rockingly . . . (SOV, p. 264).

He looked at her peeringly (LOL, p. 310).

. . . she lifted her eyes to him pleadingly . . . (LOL, p. 336).

The adverb often just repeats what the verb expresses. An eel is laid in front of the fire. The effect of light from the flames playing down the body of the eel is adequately described by "glistened" : "oilily" is superfluous. The attempt to go for effects can even lead to inaccuracy. The American did not chase the girl "laughingly". The sentence would be more correctly rendered, for example : "Once the

American chased her, laughing." Similarly, the coffin was not laid "rockingly". This suggests that the pall-bearers deliberately placed the coffin on the ground in such a manner that it rocked. All that O'Faolain wishes to say is that when the coffin was placed on the ground, the uneven surface caused the coffin to rock.

Searching for effect can be taken even further :

A string of intestines was streaking away out into the lake. Dark serpentine shapes whirled snakily in and out of the brown water. The eels had smelled the rank bait and were converging on it. (SOV, p. 250).

O'Faolain begins the paragraph by cleverly suggesting that the fowl's guts are moving out into the lake of their own volition, whereas it is the eels which have fastened on to the bait. In the next sentence three words in particular are employed to create what the author has in mind : "serpentine", "whirled", "snakily". "Serpentine" suggests cunning, underhand, whereas "snakily" refers more to the manner in which the eels moved. Yet taken together, these words try to do too much.

The consequences are not so serious in the above passage since what is being presented is not essential to the story. However there are occasions on which the straining for effect has a more unfortunate result :

She was the only one who spoke and it was plain from the way her attendants covered their faces with their hands that she was being ribald about each new arrival; the men knew it too, for as each one came forward on the sward, to meet the judgement of her dancing, wicked eyes, he skipped hastily into the undergrowth . . . (SOV, p. 264).

O'Faolain clearly wishes to demonstrate the indomitable spirit of the old woman. He has no intention of letting sentimentality creep into the story. He overcomes the problem by introducing humour into the burial scene. In the circumstances this is appropriate since the old woman is noted for the sharpness of her tongue. O'Faolain is not content to let the description in the first part of the paragraph stand alone. The attendants cover their faces to hide their laughter. The men are local people, mostly farm labourers. Even if the widow made a sharp remark, would such men be likely to "skip"? They might turn away quickly, or jerk their heads back, but they would certainly not jump. Nor would they "skip into the undergrowth". They would move away and stand on one side of the grave.

There is even a discrepancy in the sequence of events. The text reads, "for *as* each one came forward . . . to meet . . . he skipped hastily into the undergrowth." It would surely be more logical for the sentence to run : "After each one had come forward on the sward to meet the judgement of her dancing, wicked eyes, he skipped . . .", since he would have no reason to react until he had heard what the woman said.

The figures are silhouetted on the bare hillside. The writer presents the scene as if he were an onlooker watching from some distance. That is why the movements are described and why no words spoken by the widow are audible. The inappropriateness of the phrase : ". . . skipped hastily into the undergrowth . . ." make a situation which through humour was to have stressed the widow's spirit merely ludicrous.

The use of inaccurate or distractive metaphor in the presentation of character has been examined earlier in the chapter. For example, the widow – a tiny shrunken creature – was described as "lumbering" up the stairs. The cumulative effect of such imagery on important characters and on events which are essential must necessarily weaken the overall success of a story.

METAPHOR AND PERSONAL CLICHÉ

It has been argued so far that metaphor should help to dilate meaning, that the associations it introduces should clarify and enrich. If a writer does not keep his attention fixed firmly on what he wishes to achieve by means of imagery, he may find himself working at the level of pure metaphor.

In the case of O'Faolain it is sometimes possible to follow the process whereby metaphor slowly becomes separate from the objects which it should be illustrating.

In "Midsummer Night Madness", Henn's long neck is frequently mentioned. To suggest that this is a graceful attribute, O'Faolain brings in metaphor :

As their eyes met his lean neck (originally "the swan's") curved up to her lovingly. (MNM, *FS*, p. 17).

. . . smiling quizzically down on them from his swan's neck. (MNM, p. 31).

This may not be very original metaphor, but what lies behind it is easily understood. What happens in later stories?

. . . she held up her long lovely neck suspiciously and decided to be incredulous. ("The Trout", p. 228).

The verb-construction "held up" suggests that Julia is actually holding her neck in her hand.

In a story from *I Remember! I Remember!* a young woman's neck is described twice on the same page :

. . . her neck straight as a swan's . . .
Her head swayed feebly on her long neck like a daffodil in a slight wind. ("A Shadow, Silent as a Cloud", p. 40).

In the first instance, presumably the grace and straightness of the girl's neck are to be emphasized. In the second, if one interprets what is said literally, one will have the impression of a monstrously long neck. The simile acts as a distractor.

Sometimes there may even be a kind of arbitrary transference of metaphor from story to story, so that the metaphor becomes autonomous, and as a result, distractive :

"Oh, then, there was a rise," she cried. "I saw their silver bellies shining as they leaped." ("Midsummer Night Madness", *FS*, p. 18).
. . . the fish panting in his tiny prison, his silver stomach going up and down like an engine. ("The Trout", *FS*, p. 229).
. . . his silver belly went up and down. (TT, p. 229).
. . . with the sobs his tummy went in and out like an engine. ("The Judas Touch", *FS*, p. 222).
. . . the fish . . . was panting like an engine (TT, p. 230).

In "Midsummer Night Madness" O'Faolain's diction was still very much influenced by traditional Romantic language, so that the adoption of an adjective like "silver" does not surprise. Indeed it can be justified. It is possible that as the trout jumped from the water, they did appear to be silver. The word "bellies" was deliberately chosen for reasons of irony since the girl is pregnant :

"Ooh !" mocked Stevey. "Bellies ! Naughty word ! Ooh !" (MNM, p. 18).

In "The Judas Touch" the little boy's stomach is described as going "in and out like an engine". Even if the simile is somewhat far-fetched, it does add to the meaning in that it stresses the convulsive movement of the boy's stomach as he cries. Is it not reasonable to assume that this figure of speech has then been taken over and applied to another object, but this time the writer's eye has been more on the metaphor than on the object to which it refers?

A somewhat similar process may be observed with words which in the course of time have become "personal cliché". For example, "white", which traditionally implies purity, chasteness. Even at the time when O'Faolain started to write, using the word in this manner would have been considered cliché.

Presumably with the intention of adding new meaning to the expression, O'Faolain continues to employ "white", often applying it to something to which it does not belong. In early stories, the adjective generally serves to show the colour of something. The gypsy girl (MNM, *FS*, p. 22) was "white to her teeth", or an English girl, ". . . her white teeth showing". ("Egotists", *A Purse of Coppers*, p. 87).

Later, the whitness is qualified :

. . . her teeth were as white . . . as snow on a tree. (*Come Back to Erin*, p. 90).

. . . teeth as white as a hound's ("The Man Who Invented Sin", *FS*, p. 171).

His teeth were as white as paper. ("An Irish Colleen", *The Heat of the Sun*, p. 198).

Often the adjective moves into the realm of pure metaphor :

He gave her his white grin. ("Before the Daystar", *The Heat of the Sun*, p. 152).

. . . white-mouthed, red-lipped, tongue-showing like a cat. ("One Night in Turin", *I Remember! I Remember!*, p. 136).

She . . . smiled her smile that was whiter than the whites of her eyes, . . . (LOL, p. 310).

She turned her head slowly and by the dashboard light he saw her white smile. (LOL, p. 335).

Clearly O'Faolain, while thinking of teeth, has gone on to apply their colour to the mouth. It must be doubtful if the general reader would be able to work that out. What, furthermore, would the reader make of the statement that "her smile was whiter than the whites of her eyes."?

Sometimes the result is mere illogicality :

The open mouth showed fine white teeth smiling down at them.

("No Country for Old Men", *I Remember! I Remember!*, p. 175).

She laughed down at him with white teeth. ("The Talking Trees", *The Talking Trees*, p. 94).

As a contrast now, two examples of description which are clear and meaningful :

I saw the little broken corner of her tooth. ("Fugue", *FS*, p. 49).

His teeth were much too white to be his own. ("Dividends", *The Heat of the Sun*, p. 49).

In the first example, the young boy is looking at the girl directly. The slight imperfection of her teeth is what he notices. There is no suggestion that the girl was a perfect beauty. The second example shows O'Faolain making a very neat ironic comment. In both cases, reference to the teeth or to their colour is of relevance to the story.

Sometimes a metaphorical construction is transmuted in the course of one and the same story, to become more and more exaggerated. For example in consecutive stories, "£1000 for Rosebud" and "An Irish Colleen", the voice of a man who is talking to the girl he loves :

He would simply utter her rosy name from the depth of his throat . . . ("£1000 for Rosebud", *The Heat of the Sun*, p. 172).

. . . he had asked throatily. (Ibid, p. 172).

Then he got throaty. (Ibid, p. 177).

. . . he muttered throatily . . . (Ibid, p. 193).

He chuckled down in his throat . . . ("An Irish Colleen", *The Heat of the Sun*, p 209).

He chuckled his throat smile . . . (Ibid, p. 216).

He gave his sour, throaty chuckle. (Ibid, p. 218).

He throated like a wood-pigeon. (Ibid, p. 219).

There is also a tendency for vague descriptive words noted in early stories, for example, "rich", to appear :

I thought her blue apron drooped over her too rich, too wide hips. ("Midsummer Night Madness", *FS*, p. 7).

. . . a rich, mature beauty with an Italian-style figure. ("One Night in Turin", *I Remember! I Remember!*, p. 130).

A fat old woman in black, rich-breasted, gray-haired . . . (LOL, p. 317).

or combinations of slang with strange, animal comparisons :

. . . Nancy Coogan, big, bustling, bosomy, bare-armed and with a laugh like a thunderclap . . . ("Love's Young Dream", *I Remember! I Remember!*, p. 66).

. . . he watched her buttocks swaying provocatively around the corner of Kildare Street. ("A Dear Cert", *The Talking Trees*, p. 25).

He glanced covertly at her beam. (Ibid, p. 27).

corner of Kildare Street. ("A Dead Cert", *The Talking Trees*, p. 147).

He observed that she had eyes as big as a cow, eyelids as sleepy as a cow, soft hair the colour of a Jersey cow, and that she was very well made around the brisket. (Ibid, p. 151).

The one dressed in red like a robin redbreast, all bosom and bum . . . ("Liars", *The Talking Trees*, p. 102).

. . . a frieze of golden youths in bottomy bikinis. (Ibid, p. 116).

A dark, sturdy, bosomy, bottomy, boss of a robin who would spend her life . . . ("Thieves", *The Talking Trees*, p. 226).

Obviously many of the adjectives quoted are brought in for humorous effect. There is nevertheless a sense that sometimes, as a result of the sheer number of descriptive terms, they have taken on an existence of their own which is quite separate from the objects to which they happen to be attached. It is difficult, for example, to know what is : "a dark, sturdy, bosomy, bottomy, boss of a robin . . ."

Certain archaic expressions will be found to recur in the stories. Two words in particular, "poll" and "maw", tend to appear in the later work in places where a simpler expression would be more natural, often, more accurate :

(opening)   . . . maw of the tunnel. (TT, p. 230).

(head/hair) . . . his cap was on his poll. (SOV, p. 248).

(chimney) . . . the brown soot of the chimney's maw. (SOV, p. 252).

(eternity) . . . but through a maw of time. (SOV, p. 260).

(entrance) . . . disappeared into the maw of the church porch. (LOL, p. 328).

The recurrent use of these two archaic expressions, as indeed of favourite verbs like "float" and "whirl", may be regarded as a personal eccentricity. Nevertheless, the appearance of archaisms can mark emotionalism on the part of the writer and a slight loss of control – for example, "lightsome" in "The Trout" – or that a story has lost momentum, or is becoming too long. For example, much of the last section of "Lovers of the Lake" is not essential. The two lovers have taken from the pilgrim island what it has to give them. Their departure from the island is really the end of the story. The long drive down the west coast of Ireland adds nothing to their knowledge of each other, or to the reader's understanding of their situation. Archaisms occur here. For example, "strand" for shore.

Elsewhere, as has already been seen in "The Silence of the Valley", archaisms may be part of a failure resulting from straining for effect. For example, in the re-appearance of adjectives which have a superfluous "y" added : "a mountainy lad" (SOV, p. 261), a "roundy black hat" (SOV, p. 260).

At the same time it is not possible to be dogmatic. There are passages in "The Silence of the Valley" (for example, the opening section) where the introduction of archaisms is justifiable. The words "plash" and "pent" discussed earlier, are clear, accurate, and full of meaningful association.

REPETITION : INTERCHANGEABILITY

The frequent recurrence of certain favourite words which are employed more and more metaphorically has already been mentioned. Sometimes isolated words or metaphors will be repeated within the same story, but applied to different objects :

> The skin of her neck was corrugated. (LOL, p. 316).
>
> The big lumbering ferryboat was approaching, its prow slapping the corrugated waves. (LOL, p. 317).
>
> . . . such a gush of affection came over her . . . (LOL, p. 325).
>
> After a while it became clear that the woman was beside herself with terror. She suddenly let it all out in a gush of exhaled smoke. (LOL, p. 327).
>
> The girl's eyes roved sadly over the lake as if she were surveying a lake of human unhappiness. (LOL, p. 328).
>
> Immediately she lay down she spiralled to the bottom of a deep lake of sleep. (LOL, p. 328).

The danger with such arbitrary application of the same words to different objects is either that the reader will become confused – it is not easy to reconcile "corrugated" skin with "corrugated" waves – , or he may become indifferent, if "gush" may indicate both the exhalation of smoke and the expression of emotion. Similarly, the

K

metaphor "lake" is used to indicate sleep and unhappiness on the same page. There is the possibility that through being employed in this undisciplined way, words may become interchangeable, and hence meaningless.

A longer passage indicates even more clearly what can happen :

> She swam into an ecstasy as rare as one of those perfect dances of her youth when she used to swing in a whirl of music, a swirl of bodies, a circling of light, floated out of her mortal frame, alone in the arms that embraced her. (LOL, p. 322).

First, Jenny "swims" into an ecstasy, which is a mixed metaphor (repeated on the following page : . . . old hermits . . . swim off into a trance . . .). Again there is illogicality. If the dance was "perfect", why, in floating "out of her mortal frame" would she be "alone"? But the passage really takes off into total metaphor with the three phrases : "a whirl of music, a swirl of bodies, a circling of lights,". The three words, "Whirl", "swirl", "circle" are more or less interchangeable. All three phrases are cliché. Placing them together does not add to or intensify the effect.

There can be no doubt that Jenny has become light-headed from lack of food and sleep. This is a situation which requires very sensitive treatment if it is not to disintegrate into emotional blur.

To see just how brilliantly O'Faolain can describe Jenny's semi-conscious state, one needs merely to look back to the beginning of the same paragraph :

> Exhaustion began to work on her mind. Objects began to disconnect, become isolated each within its own outline – now it was the pulpit, now a statue, now a crucifix. Each object took on the vividness of a hallucination. The crucifix detached itself from the wall and leaned towards her, and for a long while she saw nothing but the heavy pendent body, the staring eyes, so that when the old man at her side let his head sink over on her shoulder and then woke up with a start she felt him no more than if they were two fishes touching in the sea. Bit by bit the incantations drew her in; sounds came from her mouth; prayers flowed between her and those troubled eyes that fixed hers. (LOL, p. 322).

O'Faolain is looking directly at and through Jenny. He takes the reader into Jenny's mind, into her dream state where solid objects begin to detach themselves. This is imaginative writing which expands the sense, adds depth to the scene and to the reader's awareness of a state of mind. The description is precise even when referring to the imprecise : "Each object took on the vividness of a hallucination." Instead of slipping into the vacuity of suggestive cliché, O'Faolain sticks to the solid objects around Jenny and brings these in to conjure up a sense of disembodiment. That is where the paragraph should have ended. Up to this point there is evidence of control, of metaphor illustrating, clarifying, and discreetly strengthening what the writer is trying to express.

Conclusion

In this study I have deliberately worked within very narrow terms of reference. It would therefore be inappropriate at the end to attempt a general summing-up of O'Faolain's achievements. O'Faolain has written short stories, novels, biography, history, drama and literary criticism. Apart from brief references to the novels, I have concentrated on the short stories, selecting from a large number, merely eight for detailed examination.

By careful analysis of descriptive techniques and diction in stories published over a long period I have tried to demonstrate how O'Faolain slowly worked his way towards a style of his own. I have suggested that this development proceeded in three stages.

I began with a discussion of the first stories in which, for all their Romantic, sometimes uncontrolled exuberance of language, O'Faolain still generally succeeds in employing language which is in harmony with what the stories are about. This was followed by a chapter in which a later story ("Admiring the Scenery") was examined. Here it was possible to discern, in the economy of language, in the tightness of control, in the exclusion of the extraneous and in the concentration on the essential, both O'Faolain's early mastery of his art and also assimilation of other models.

The verbal asceticism was seen to ease in stories which came after *A Purse of Coppers*. In "Lady Lucifer" and "Up the Bare Stairs" (discussed in the third chapter), a seemingly casual, often deliberately colloquial diction was noted. This manner appears to be the final stage in a development which has given the reader more and more opportunity to work out for himself what a story expresses, through the medium of what I have called mediacy.

In the early stories, the writer was so personally involved that this tends to be reflected in the diction, with the result that the reader is constantly being forced to react in a certain way. Even in the stories in *A Purse of Coppers*, where rigorous control was exercised, the point the author wishes to make, for example in "Admiring the Scenery", is cunningly referred to in ways which the casual reader is unlikely to notice – a whole series of hidden persuaders. In the later stories, O'Faolain is content to let the stories "tell themselves". The reader is no longer being gently or otherwise led to accept the author's viewpoint. All three methods are successfully deployed by O'Faolain.

In the final chapter I have attempted to discuss certain problems and possible limitations in O'Faolain's descriptive techniques and diction. My main concern throughout this study has been to show that words must have a connection with the objects they are to describe, reflect on, or illustrate. I have argued that where such links can be proven, a true fusion of word and content is established. Where the writer loses himself in metaphor, or where his verbal camera becomes unfocused, this will be reflected in the words he chooses. Metaphor becomes distractive, separated from what it is to intensify. The result of misapplied metaphor can at worst be not only distraction, but total destruction of what the writer has set out to achieve.

Bibliography

I. SEAN O'FAOLAIN – MAJOR WORKS

Lyrics and Satires from Tom Moore. Dublin : Cuala Press, 1929.

Midsummer Night Madness and Other Stories. London : Jonathan Cape, 1932.

The Life Story of Eamon De Valera. Dublin : Talbot Press, 1933.

A Nest of Simple Folk. New York : The Viking Press, 1934.

Constance Markievicz, or The Average Revolutionary: A Biography. London : Jonathan Cape, 1934.

Bird Alone. London : Jonathan Cape, 1936.

A Purse of Coppers: Short Stories. London : Jonathan Cape, 1937.

The Autobiography of Theobald Wolfe Tone. London : Thomas Nelson, 1937.

She Had to Do Something: A Comedy in Three Acts. London : Jonathan Cape, 1938.

King of the Beggars: A Life of Daniel O'Connell. New York : The Viking Press, 1938.

Come Back to Erin. New York : The Viking Press, 1940.

An Irish Journey. London : Longmans Green, 1940.

The Great O'Neill: A Biography of Hugh O'Neill, Earl of Tyrone. 1850–1916. New York : Duell, Sloan & Pearce, 1942.

The Story of Ireland. London : William Collins, 1943.

Teresa, and Other Stories. London : Jonathan Cape, 1947.

The Irish: A Character Study. New York : The Devin-Adair Co., 1948.

The Short Story. London : William Collins, 1948.

The Man Who Invented Sin, and Other Stories. New York : The Devin-Adair Co., 1949.

A Summer in Italy. London : Eyre and Spottiswoode, 1949.

Newman's Way: The Odyssey of John Henry Newman. London : Longmans Green, 1952.

South to Sicily. London : William Collins, 1953.

The Vanishing Hero: Studies in Novelists of the Twenties. London : Eyre and Spottiswoode, 1956.

The Finest Stories of Sean O'Faolain. Boston : Little, Brown and Company, 1957.

Short Stories: A Study in Pleasure. Edited by Sean O'Faolain. Boston : Little, Brown and Company, 1961.

I Remember! I Remember! Boston : Little, Brown and Company, 1961.

Vive Moi! Boston : Little, Brown and Company, 1964.

The Heat of the Sun: Stories and Tales. Boston : Little, Brown and Company, 1966.

The Talking Trees and Other Stories. London : Jonathan Cape, 1971.

Foreign Affairs. Lodon : Constable, 1976.

II. SECONDARY LITERATURE ON THE SHORT STORY AND ON SEAN O'FAOLAIN

(a) *Books*

Babel, Isaac. *You Must Know Everything.* London : Joanthan Cape, 1970.

Baker, Carlos. *Hemingway: The Writer as Artist.* Princeton : Princeton University Press, 1970.

Baker, Carlos, ed. *Hemingway and his Critics.* New York : Hill and Wang, 1961.

Beachcroft, T. O. *The Modest Art: A Survey of the Short Story in English.* London : Oxford University Press, 1968.

Bates, H. E. *The Modern Short Story.* Boston : The Writer Inc., 1941.

Bowen, Elizabeth. *Collected Impressions.* London : Longmans Green, 1950.

Buchloh, Paul G., ed. *Amerikanische Erzählungen von Hawthorn bis Salinger.* Neumünster : Karl Wachholtz Verlag, 1968.

Bungert, Hans, ed. *Die Amerikanische Short Story: Theorie einer Entwicklung.* Darmstadt : Wissenschaftliche Buchgesellschaft, 1972.

Current-Garcia, Eugine & Patrick, Walton R., eds. *What Is the Short Story?* Glenview, Ill. : Scott, Foresmann, 1961.

Dalton, Pauline. *The Narrative Art of Sean O'Faolain.* Diss. Leeds, 1972.

Dockrell-Grünberg, Susanne. *Studien zur Struktur Moderner Anglo-Irischer Short Stories.* Diss. Tübingen, 1967.

Doyle, Paul A. *Sean O'Faolain.* New York : Twayne Publishers, 1968.

Freese, Peter. *Die Amerikanische Kurzgeschichte seit 1945.* Frankfurt/Main : Athenäum Verlag, 1974.

Friedland, Louis S., ed. *Chekhov Letters on the Short Story, the Drama, and Other Literary Topics.* London : Vision Press, 1965.

Goetsch, Paul. *Studien und Materialien zur Short Story.* Frankfurt/
Main : Verlag Moritz Diesterweg, 1971.

Göller, Karl Heinz and Hoffmann, Gerhard, eds. *Die englische
Kurzgeschichte.* Düsseldorf : August Bagel Verlag, 1973.

Harmon, Maurice. *Sean O'Faolain: A Critical Introduction.*
London : University of Notre Dame Press, 1966.

Hemingway, Ernest. *Death in the Afternoon.* London : Penguin,
1966.

Kast, Hans. *George Moore und Frankreich.* Diss. Tübingen, 1962.

Kiely, Benedict. *Modern Irish Fiction: A Critiqu*e. Dublin : Golden
Eagle Books, 1950.

Kilchenmann, Ruth. *Die Kurzgeschichte.* Stuttgart : W. Kohl-
hammer, 1967.

Maugham, W. Somerset. *The Summing Up.* London : William
Heinemann, 1938.

Maugham, W. Somerset. *A Writer's Notebook.* London : William
Heinemann, 1949.

Maupassant, Guy de. *Pierre et Jean, and Selected Short Stories*
(Introduction). New York : Bantam Books, 1959.

Murphy, Katherine A. *Imaginative Vision and Story Art in Three
Irish Writers: Sean O'Faolain, Mary Lavin, Frank O'Connor.* Diss.
Dublin, 1967/68.

O'Connor, Frank. *The Mirror in the Roadway.* London : Hamish
Hamilton, 1957.

O'Connor, Frank. *The Lonely Voice.* New York : Bantam Books,
1968.

O'Donnell, Donat. *Maria Cross.* New York : Oxford University
Press, 1952.

Pianezza, Annie. *The World of Sean O'Faolain's Stories.* Diss. Lille,
1969.

Rohner, Ludwig. *Theorie der Kurzgeschichte.* Frankfurt/Main :
Athenäum Verlag, 1973.

Trautmann, Joanne. *Counterparts: The Stories and Traditions of
Frank O'Connor and Sean O'Faolain.* Diss. Indiana, 1967.

Wright, Austen McGiffert. *The American Short Story in the Twenties.* Chicago : University of Chicago Press, 1964.

(b) *Articles*

Beck, Warren. "Art and Formula in the Short Story". *College
English,* V, 1943/4, 55–62.

Braybrooke, Neville. "Sean O'Faolain : A Study". *The Dublin
Magazine,* XXXI, April–June 1955, 22–27.

Cantwell, Robert. "Poet of the Irish Revolution". *New Republic*, LXXVII, January 24, 1934, 313–314.

Diers, Richard. "On Writing : An Interview with Sean O'Faolain". *Mademoiselle*, LVI, March 1963, 151, 209–215.

Doderer, K. "Die angelsächsische Short Story und die deutsche Kurzgeschichte". *Die Neueren Sprachen*, II, 1953, 417–424.

Farrell, James T. "A Harvest of O'Faolain". *New Republic*, CXXXVI, June 17, 1957, 19–20.

Finn, James. "High Standards and High Achievements". *Commonweal*, LXVI, July 26, 1957, 428–429.

Gregory, Horace. "Imaginative Tales". *Saturday Review*, XL, May 25, 1957, 15–16.

Gullason, Thomas H. "The Short Story : An Underrated Art". *Studies in Short Fiction*, II, 1964/5, 13–31.

Hanley, Katherine. "The Short Stories of Sean O'Faolain : Theory and Practice". *Eire*, 6 : 3, Fall 1971, 3–11.

Höllerer, Walter. "Die kurze Form der Prosa". *Akzente*, IX, 1962, 226–245.

Hopkins, Robert H. "The Pastoral Mode of Sean O'Faolain's 'The Silence of the Valley' ". *Studies in Short Fiction*, I, Winter 1964, 93–98.

Kelleher, John V. "Loneliness Is the Key". *The New York Times Book Review*, May 12, 1957, pp. 5, 23.

Kelleher, John V. "Sean O'Faolain". *Atlantic Monthly*, CXCIX, May 1957, 67–69.

McMahon, Sean. "O My Youth, O My Country". *Eire*, 6 : 3, Fall 1971, 145–156.

Mertner, Edgar. "Zur Theorie der Short Story in England und Amerika". *Anglia*, LXV, 1941, 188–205.

Nichols, Lewis. "Talk with Mr O'Faolain". *The New York Times Book Review*, May 12, 1957, 26–27.

O'Faolain, Sean. "Cruelty and Beauty of Words". *Virginia Quarterly Review*, IV, April, 1928, 208–225.

O'Faolain, Sean. "Literary Provincialism". *Commonweal*, XVIII, December 21, 1932, 214–215.

O'Faolain, Sean. "Written Speech". *Commonweal*, XXVII, November 5, 1937, 35–36.

O'Faolain, Sean. "The Secret of the Short Story". *United Nations World*, III, March 1949, 37–38.

O'Faolain, Sean. "On Being an Irish Writer". *Commonweal*, LVIII, July 10, 1953, 339–341.

O'Faolain, Sean. "Are You Writing a Short Story". *The Listener*, LIX, February 13, 1958, 282–283.

O'Faolain, Sean. "Writer at Work". *St Stephen's* (Dublin), Michaelmas, 1962, pp. 25–26.

Pritchett, V. S. "O'Faolain's Troubles". *New Statesman*, LXX, August 13, 1965, 219–220.

Saroyan, William. "The Unholy Word". *The Bell*, XV, October, 1947, 33–37.

Welty, Eudora. "The Reading and Writing of Short Stories". *Atlantic Monthly*, CLXXXIII, 1949, ii, 54–58, iii, 46–49.

West, Ray B. "The Modern Short Story and the Highest Forms of Art". *English Journal*, XLVI, December 1957, 531–539.